Mimi
Tokyo Paris

A Tale of Love and Globalization

Junichi Nishimura

iUniverse, Inc.
Bloomington

Mimi Tokyo Paris
A Tale of Love and Globalization

Copyright © 2011 Junichi Nishimura

This is a work of fiction. All of the characters, names, incidents, organizations, and dialogue in this novel are either the products of the author's imagination or are used fictitiously.

iUniverse books may be ordered through booksellers or by contacting:

iUniverse
1663 Liberty Drive
Bloomington, IN 47403
www.iuniverse.com
1-800-Authors (1-800-288-4677)

Because of the dynamic nature of the Internet, any web addresses or links contained in this book may have changed since publication and may no longer be valid. The views expressed in this work are solely those of the author and do not necessarily reflect the views of the publisher, and the publisher hereby disclaims any responsibility for them.

Any people depicted in stock imagery provided by Thinkstock are models, and such images are being used for illustrative purposes only.

Certain stock imagery © Thinkstock.

ISBN: 978-1-4620-0560-4 (pbk)
ISBN: 978-1-4620-0561-1 (clth)
ISBN: 978-1-4620-0562-8 (ebk)

Library of Congress Control Number: 2011904279

Printed in the United States of America

iUniverse rev. date: 04/27/2011

Mimi

"Konichiwa"! My name is Mimi. For eight years now, I have been working at Doutor, a Japanese version of Starbucks coffee shop. I am proud to work at a Japanese company, even if it is a copycat of the original.

Café latte. Mache latte. Hotto. Shorto. Milano sando, A, B, C. Germand'og. That's the daily routine.

Like lots of Japanese, we live in the underworld, in the basement of an office building, in the midst of a shopping arcade. People are always rushing by on the way to or from the metro, and some of them pop in for a coffee.

Fortunately, we don't have to be smiley and friendly all the time to our customers like they are at Starbucks. Our customers are more mature. They come for the coffee and food, and to be left in peace. They don't come to Doutor to have an experience!

I am rather "TJ", typically Japanese. I am a perfectionist, rather meticulous and finicky actually. My daily dream is to make the perfect café latte, full to the brim, without spilling a drop. And I then I draw a little cat using the black coffee in the foam. It's so "kawaii", or cute as you say in English.

My colleagues are lots of fun. They are mainly girls, but there are two young boys who are more feminine than us girls. Since they do not seem very virile or masculine, we call such boys "grass-eaters" ("soushoku danshi"). There are more and more boys like that in Japan today.

One of my colleagues is Chinese. She speaks perfect Japanese and English. It's a bit embarrassing because we Japanese barely speak a word of English, let alone Chinese. Actually, I picked up a bit of French at the Institut Franco Japanais in Ichigaya in Tokyo.

My Chinese colleague even uses an English first name, "Sandy". She originally came to Japan on a trainee visa. But she is not really a trainee. She does a normal job, but gets paid half the salary. It's not really fair, although she's not a perfectionist like us.

My father told me to be careful about Sandy. He's convinced that China is plotting to invade Japan in about ten years, or even less.

I am sure that I could get a better job if I tried. But I am happy here. We have lots of fun. And the customers are great, especially the Westerners who talk and flirt with us. From what I can see, however, Sandy is the only one to be invited out by a customer. Coming from northern China, she is rather tall. But she doesn't giggle all the time like we do.

In reality, there are not many other good jobs on the market these days. Everything now seems to be temporary work. You get a two month contract, and they renew it if they like you. In fact, I am not working for Doutor, I am employed by an agency that has a contract with Doutor.

My parents are pushing me to get a decent job. After all, I have a masters degree in sociology from the University of Great Wisdom (UGW) in Tokyo. Sociology is interesting, but you can't do much with that.

Anyway, I don't want to live like my parents. Dad is always at work, I never see him. In fact, I barely know him. When he is not at work, he is drinking with his colleagues. Then on the weekend he sleeps all the time.

My mother is always complaining about the smell of perfume on my father's clothes. And then the other day, I heard her yelling at him -- something about a Louis Vuitton handbag on his credit card bill. Who on earth could he have bought that for?

Anyway, my parents don't spend much time together. My mother doesn't work any more. She gave up work when she had me. We spend lots of time together as I am the only child now since my brother's suicide. When I was younger, she was really busy because she had to look after both my father's parents and her parents. What an ordeal! But now they have passed away.

These days my mother goes out a lot with her girlfriends -- shopping, restaurants and movies. I think that she spends lots of money. But she runs the household budget, and no-one knows the details. I think that she made a killing by investing on the stock exchange, but she won't talk about it. She gives my father monthly pocket money -- 50,000 yen a month. That's a lot, many husbands only get 20,000 yen. But it keeps my father off her back.

My mother also goes away on holidays with her girlfriends. One time I overheard her speaking with a girlfriend about doing vaginal steam bath treatments in Korea! It is supposed to do all sorts of things like reducing stress, fighting infections, clearing hemorrhoids, regulating menstrual cycles and aiding infertility. She is amazing! But usually she goes to Europe on holidays. I think that she also has lots of fun there too, although she doesn't talk to me about it. She certainly brings back lots of fashionable clothes and sexy underwear.

All things considered, I am happy. Living at home is easy. At the age of 30, may be I am a bit old to be living at home. But I get by quite well. I go out with my girlfriends on the weekends. I don't have a boyfriend yet. In fact, I don't like boys much. Japanese boys are so effeminate. Then there are the older salarymen who chase young girls. They're terrible.

Junichi Nishimura

The other day, I went out to the movies with an American boy. He touched my legs when the lights went out. I didn't know what to do. I am still a virgin. I don't even feel sexy.

Anyway, he didn't push. He's a nice boy. I hope that he calls me again. I would like to get married and have a family one day. Too many Japanese girls wait too long and miss the boat.

In fact, meeting him really made me think. I hope that I am not wasting my life.

Miyuki

I am Miyuki. My life is so hard. I sell newspapers from a little stand at a Tokyo metro station. I spend six hours every day locked up in this little stand. Now I have some idea about solitary confinement in a prison.

No-one talks to me. Japanese people don't talk to strangers. Also, they would think of me as being the lowest of the low.

People buy lots of newspapers and manga, the Japanese cartoons. But the men love most of all the magazines with photos of lightly clad school girls showing their underpants. The funny thing is that none of them look at me, although I think that I am rather pretty. May be it is because I am just over 40 years old. Japanese men want young girls under 20 years old, preferably dressed up as school girls.

I am always so tired. I start work at 6.00. But to arrive there on time, I have to wake up at 4.00. I get ready and then have a one and a half hour commute.

But it's worse than that. I only earn 110,000 yen a month in this terrible job. So I have to work in a supermarket in the evening too. That helps me barely survive.

It's not fair, you know. I used to have an office job. It wasn't a great job. But I could make ends meet. My boss was terrible. He had a violent temper. He would get so angry and lose his temper. He would tell us to do one thing, and then the opposite thing. He would blame us for everything. And then he would threaten to fire us. In Japanese we call this "powahara". This means "power harassment".

In Japan, people talk a lot about powahara, but nothing is ever done about this. The boss is always right, especially if it is a man.

Then there is "sekuhara". This is Japanese for sexual harassment. This is what happened to me. The boss used to touch me and push his body up against mine. I tried to push him away, but it was always difficult. I am strong. But he was stronger. It got worse and worse. He wouldn't stop.

One day, he said that if I didn't have sex with him, he would fire me. I couldn't take it any longer. So I left.

My former female colleagues don't like me anymore. They are jealous of the fact that I was brave enough to leave. They are also upset because the boss is now picking on them.

Even though my life is difficult, I have regained my self respect. I live alone with my cats. Actually one died last month, but I still have the other one.

Living alone is kinda sad. But I do feel free, although I am always tired. My daily commute is such an ordeal. People packed in the train like sardines, pushing and shoving. Although the men are terrible, the women are almost as bad.

One day in a crowded train, I suddenly felt a hand rush under my skirt and push into my panties. I instantly felt all hot and sweaty. I can not describe my feelings to tell the truth.

After a moment's hesitation, I screamed "groper, molester". That's what you are supposed to yell.

No-one in the crowd reacted. A man quickly motioned to run away. I grabbed his arm so tightly he could not get away. I learn self defense and judo, and have a very strong grip. The more he tried to get away, the more I held tight. I dragged him off the train at the next stop, which was only minutes away.

He broke down in tears. He begged me for forgiveness. He was probably in his fifties, a good ten years older than me. He looked perfectly normal, probably a successful salaryman.

He cried and cried and cried. He pleaded again for forgiveness. He rambled on about his important job, his family, his pressures and so on.

I began to feel sorry for him. He actually seemed rather nice. He was tall, handsome and elegantly dressed.

I invited him for a coffee. He said that he did not know what came over him. In the crowded train, with all those bodies crammed together, flesh against flesh, he just lost control. Then he started talking about his family. His son had committed suicide, and his daughter Mimi is wasting her time working in a Doutor café.

I really felt sorry for him. I guess we can all do silly things in a moment of weakness. We agreed to meet again tomorrow.

Mimi

Hi, I'm Mimi from Doutor, back to tell the next piece of my story.

After more than eight years working away in the coffee shop, I had enough savings to plan a trip to Paris. I convinced my girlfriend Momo to come along with me. We Japanese girls all dream of going to Paris, the "city of light". I will be able to use my French, even though it has become a bit rusty.

Paris is of course the home of the great museums of the world with their impressionist paintings. I love Monet's water lilies most of all. I want go to the Musee d'Orsay, but I especially want to go to the Musee Marmottan. I have heard that it is a cute little museum on the outskirts of Paris with Monet's best water lily paintings. Then there is the Orangerie Museum with its immense mural water lilies. And last but not least is Giverny, Monet's home where he painted most of his water lilies.

There are lots of other things that I would like to see in Paris. But really, it's Monet's water lilies most of all. There is something erotic about them. I often dream of floating nude in a pond of water lilies, and feeling the flowers caress my body. The climax is when one water lily lands on my sweet spot ("schweetu-spotto" in Japanese). I first had that sensation when I visited Chichu Art Museum on Naoshima Island.

I don't know what it was. There is something about the natural light, and the atmosphere created by Monet's five water lily paintings at Chichu. I read that the size of the room, its design, and the materials used were all selected to integrate Monet's works with the surrounding space. Amazing. I was seduced even before I entered the Museum. That island is so beautiful. Somehow art and nature always transport me into a fantasy world.

There are of course lots of other things I want to see in Paris. The architecture. The shops with all the fashions and luxury products. Then there are the chateaux of the Loire Valley, not to mention Le Corbusier. His architecture is so Japanese.

All things considered, Japan and France have had a longtime love affair. We are two cultures that appreciate refinement.

So, off we went to Paris. To get into a French mood as soon as possible, Momo and I flew Air France. But as soon as we got on the plane, I noticed something was strange. The air hostesses were beautiful, but very arrogant and condescending to the Japanese passengers. I don't why. We Japanese are not like that. For us, service must be perfect. And the male flight stewards were cocky and flirting with all the young Japanese passengers. One of them – "please call me Pierre" -- kept touching me on the shoulder. We Japanese don't touch each other, especially in public. I was confused, because it gave me goose bumps.

A long while after takeoff, the dinner arrived. It sounded so exotic and delicious – confit de canard or bœuf bourguignon. I took confit de canard. But the food was cold, and the meat was tough. I didn't understand. The French flight staff didn't seem to care.

Being Japanese, we were too shy to complain to the French staff, so we called over a Japanese hostess and told her. She agreed. She said that Air France is like that. She only stays with Air France because it has a good pension system, better than Japan Airlines.

We didn't really care. All we wanted to do was to get to Paris. I hadn't paid much attention to the flight schedule when I booked the ticket. I was just thinking of Monet. But we arrived at 4.00 in the morning.

Our hotel recommended that we take a taxi from the airport rather than the Paris trains. I was so excited to take a French taxi. Would they be like our Japanese taxis with automatically opening doors and drivers with white gloves?

What a shock! When we got through customs, we were instantly approached by an African looking man offering us his private taxi. "Mesdemoiselles, come with me." I had read about this in a book, but didn't believe it until I saw it. So we ran away from him and eventually found the "official" taxi stand.

I expected to be greeted politely by a nice old taxi driver like in Tokyo. I have read that the average age of Tokyo taxi drivers is 69. To us, they are grandfather figures. Our Paris taxi driver was very dark and strange looking. I think that he might have been Arab, although I have never really seen one before. He seemed to drive for hours, and round and round in circles. I had never been to Paris before, but I am sure that we passed the same red-looking café several times. In the end, the bill was over 100 euros when we arrived at 5.30 am. According to my Japanese guide book, it should only have cost 55 euros.

We were so tired when we arrived at the hotel. All I wanted to do was go to bed. We were told that we could not check in until 2.00 pm, and that anyway the hotel was too full to give us a room before. We could have breakfast but it would not be served until 7.30 am.

So we walked out in to the street in search of a café. There must be some Doutor cafes somewhere in Paris. Or even McDonalds, they are open 24 hours a day in Tokyo. We found something that looked like a café. It was full of smoke, men were drinking. There were even a couple of dogs by the bar.

I had always dreamed of having a café au lait and croissant in Paris. It took ages for the waiter to understand me, but eventually he did. When the café au lait arrived, it was OK. But the croissant was hard and stale. The waiter explained that today's croissants had not yet arrived, they arrive directly from the baker at 6.30. Our croissants were left over from yesterday.

We went back to the hotel to wait for the day to start. It was still only 6.15 am. As we were sitting there, I started to feel dizzy and nauseous, my head was spinning, and then I think I must have fainted.

As I learnt later, Momo asked the hotel for help. They just called a taxi which took me to a hospital called Hotel-Dieu. It's very strange, I think that it means God's Hotel.

Anyway, when I came to, I was in a bed in a big room with lots of other people. Nurses were running everywhere yelling at each other. Most of the nurses were black or dark-looking like our taxi driver. I couldn't understand what they were saying, although I thought I heard something like "Syndrome de Paris". What could that be?

Sandy

My name is Sandy, and I work at Doutor with Mimi who you have already met.

In fact, I am also a Chinese student here in Japan. I am studying economics at the University of Great Wisdom. I have a Japanese scholarship. The Japanese government is desperate to give scholarships to Chinese students to improve relations between our countries. So they gave me one, even though I was already here in Japan as a trainee at Doutor. In reality, most Chinese students prefer to go to America.

In the past, these Japanese scholarships were very generous, but the Japanese government has cut back the benefits because of its national debt problems. In fact, it's a bit strange for a Chinese girl like me to be accepting a scholarship from Japan when the country has so much debt, whereas China is simply rolling in money.

I work at Doutor to make some extra money. I am the only foreigner at our coffee shop. My colleagues are very nice and friendly. They don't seem to hold a grudge against me because the Chinese and Japanese governments seem to be fighting all the time. You can't be sure however. The Japanese will never say what they really feel.

In fact, relations between China and Japan are pretty tense at the moment. The Japanese coastguard arrested a Chinese fisherman and his crew when they wandered into Japanese waters near the Senkaku

Islands. You can never tell who is guilty in these affairs. But you should never start World War 3 over such a tiny thing like this.

When the Japanese coastguard arrested the fishing ship, they could have given the fishermen a spanking and sent them back to China. But no, they held on to the captain 17 days. For we Chinese, this was a humiliation, especially since we claim these islands as our own. We gave the Japanese government plenty of warnings but they still held on to the ship's captain. It was only when Premier "grandpa" Wen Jiabao stepped into the affair with Hilary Clinton, that the Japanese government let the captain go.

It was so stupid. I heard that the Chinese and the former Japanese government had a gentleman's agreement to not arrest Chinese fishermen straying into these waters. But this new Democratic Party of Japan government is so incompetent.

I have to admit however that the Chinese government is sometimes a bit naughty. They believe that all the countries around China are part of its area of influence. This is how it was before the Westerners came to humiliate China in the 19th century. All our neighboring countries recognized China as the Middle Kingdom and our emperor as having the mandate from heaven. They called it a system of suzerainty. So our government is very happy to encourage our fishermen to stray into Japanese and other foreign waters, and make our presence felt. The Americans don't like this.

At Doutor, my Japanese colleagues and I do not talk about these issues. In fact, they don't seem very interested in current affairs, although I think that they are afraid of China. The Japanese are like that. They are really inward-looking. Japanese girls only talk about fashion and makeup, and the boys don't talk at all.

Very few Japanese use Facebook. They use Japanese social networking websites, and they usually hide their real identity. How could they ever make international friends and be part of the world?

Quite frankly, my Japanese colleagues seem a bit naïve and simple. I sometimes think that Japan is more communist than China. Life seems cosy and comfortable, with no great risks and uncertainties. People in big companies have lifetime job security. Even in small companies, people never get fired. Today, more and more young kids work on short-term contracts, which makes their life precarious.

But most of these young Japanese still live with their parents who provide free accommodation, food, and even pocket money. If they ever find a romantic partner, they can go to a "love hotel" and rent a room for a few hours. But from what I can see, most Japanese kids are not too interested in sex. In fact, I read that 60 per cent of young girls have no interest in or even despise sex. That's strange. I love sex. Most Chinese girls do. Then, because of our macho Chinese men, we sometimes need to undergo hymen reconstruction surgery before we marry (just like the Arab girls!) -- although we can also achieve revirgination by buying a Chinese-made artificial hymen in a sex novelty shop.

In China, life is much tougher than in Japan. We suffered greatly through the Cultural Revolution. That broke up families, made enemies out of friends and destroyed our best and brightest who were forced to work on farms, if they were not killed. Then came Deng Xiaoping. His reforms transformed the country. They made us more free and prosperous. But the older generation like my parents could not keep up. And we all lost the security of the communist system – no more free health care and generous pensions. Today, if you want a doctor to take your case seriously, you have to give him a side payment.

I need my job at Doutor, not just for my own survival. I must send money back to my family in China. I come from the north east, a village near Shenyang. Dad used to work in a factory. But as Deng Xiaoping's reforms started to spread, the factory was closed down. Dad lost his job, and is still unemployed. He gets a small pension, but it is just peanuts. And he is not in good health any more. My mother has a little job, but she does not earn enough to survive on. So my brother and I send them money. We are a two-child family like many people from the country.

So when I put together my scholarship money and my Doutor salary, I have enough to live on and to send money to my family. Working at Doutor takes time away from studies. But quite honestly, courses at Japanese universities are not very challenging. That's especially the case for courses designed for foreign students. They are basically a diplomatic gesture to developing countries. It's not like that in China. Our big universities are very high-powered – universities like Peking, Tsinghua, Fudan and Nankai.

I heard through some Chinese friends that the best way to earn quick money in Japan is by doing massages. In Japan, they have all sorts of massages – normal, sensual, erotic and super sexy – and as you climb this scale you get more money.

I'm not a virgin, but I don't want to be a prostitute either. So, I recently found an agency where I can do normal and sensual massages. This is what I do on Friday and Saturday evenings. I don't tell anyone because in fact it's rather strange.

What an eye-opener on Japanese society! Chinese men are pretty weird, but Japanese men take the cake. They all want quirky massages. Japanese men are all rather strange, I think.

There is one who wants me to shave his body, especially all around his genitals. And as I am doing this, he masturbates. It's a bit messy, and I have to be careful not to cut him, although he seems to get excited by the pain of being cut and seeing blood.

Then there is another one who wants me to dress up like a hairdresser. He has all the clothes, and the hairdressing scissors and so on. So I dress up, and then cut his hair, while he is sitting there nude masturbating himself.

And then there is another who loves masochism. He asks me to whip him with his belt while he is sitting there nude, masturbating himself. As the whipping starts to break his skin and blood appears, he starts yelling "Hiddey, Hiddey, Hiddey…".

It is all rather strange. But the most strange thing is that they don't touch me. They don't want sex me with me. They don't even want to see my body.

I don't understand. It must be all in their imagination.

Anyway, my goal is to make money. If I make enough money, I could start a travel agency in China. Lots of Chinese people now want to visit Japan.

I could do a good business with them, using all the contacts I have made in Japan. I am sure that I could succeed. I would certainly have no competition from Japanese people. They don't have any business sense like us Chinese. They are good at making things. Japan is a nation of craftsmen.

Mimi

Hi, it's Mimi, I'm just about to check out from the Hotel Dieu.

The French doctors and nurses kept me under medication and observation for ten days. They said that I had a severe case of Paris Syndrome. They also this that this was compounded by extreme fatigue and stress. They advised me to relax a little, to let go. Also, I must confess that I was menstruating when I arrived in Paris. On the first day, I always lose a lot of blood and am very run down.

Apparently many young Japanese girls suffer from the Paris Syndrome. We have a romantic, idealized image of Paris. And somehow, Paris does not always live up to our expectations. Arriving as we did at 4.00 in the morning does not help. We were already under pressure, with so many things to do in our four day stay.

The doctors recommended that I stay in Paris for another couple of weeks, and check in with them once a day. While many patients get better immediately, some can suffer relapses and others can develop real psychoses.

The Japanese Embassy in Paris, which is not that far along from the Hotel Dieu, has a 24 hour hotline for Japanese tourists like me. The attaché for social affairs, Takahashi-san, also recommended that I stay on for a while. He has seen many cases like me. He also said that the Hotel Dieu is the best place in the world for treating Paris Syndrome, with both excellent medical and psychological services.

What's more the Hotel Dieu is very well situated. It is just opposite Notre Dame Cathedral.

I had never heard of this Paris Syndrome before, so I decided to do a quick search on the Internet in a cyber-cafe. Apparently the Paris Syndrome was first reported in a French psychiatry journal by A. Viala and others in 2004. But to my great surprise, I found all sorts of travellers' syndromes like the Stockholm Syndrome, Lima Syndrome, Diogenes Syndrome, Jerusalem Syndrome, Capgras Delusion, Fregoli Delusion, Cotard Delusion or Reduplicative Paramnesia. It seems that only Japanese girls are struck down by the Paris Syndrome!

But what intrigued me most was the Stendhal Syndrome. So I thought that I should look it up at a library. Someone told me about the library called "Bibliothèque François Mitterrand", named after a former French President. Apparently the architecture style is very Japanese. What's more, it's quite close to Chinatown. I would love to eat some rice and dumplings!

So, off I went to this Bibliothèque François Mitterrand. There is a very handy metro line that takes you straight there. It looks very modern, a bit like our Nomboku line in Tokyo.

When I arrived, I was struck that the library looks like our own Prime Minister's residence. I went down into the library. The staff were actually very kind. There was a strange almost spiritual atmosphere in the library. Everyone was calm and serene. As I came to learn later on, culture is the real religion of the French elite. And everyone seemed to respond very positively to the fact that I am Japanese. I even noticed a section in the library for manga.

I found a great book on the Stendhal Syndrome. This syndrome occurs when you get a rapid heartbeat, dizziness and even hallucinations as you are looking at a wonderful piece of art. It comes from a famous French writer called Stendhal who was knocked out by the beauty of Florence. In fact, Stendhal is just a pen name, his real name was Marie-Henri Beyle. Some of these French names are strange how they mix male and female names together. Anyway, Stendhal is most famous for two novels he wrote over 150 years ago called "Le Rouge et le Noir" and "La Chartreuse de Parme".

And then I found out that Stendhal also wrote a book called "On Love" which is all about the "birth of love". Falling in love is when the love object is 'crystallized' in your mind. There are four steps along the way: admiration, acknowledgement, hope and delight. I had never heard or ready anything like this in my life. The French seem really romantic.

I guess that I always had a rather sheltered existence in Japan. And I never really saw anything like love between my parents. In fact, my mother's father was my father's boss when he was young. In Japan, marriages were typically arranged through parents, sometimes through contacts made at work. My grandfather invited my father home to dinner one evening, and a few months later my parents got married.

After reading all this stuff on Stendhal, I was feeling exhausted, a bit flustered actually. As I was leaving the library, I noticed a little coffee shop. It was like Doutor, although a bit shabby and dirty. So, I sat down and had a coffee. They call it café-creme.

Then all of a sudden a French boy sat down. "Please excuse me", he said, "there are no other free tables".

"You must be Japanese", he said in a rather excitable manner. "I love manga, and Japanese cuisine." He kept rambling on and on.

"I know the best Japanese ramen soup restaurants in Paris", he said. "Let's meet for lunch tomorrow. My name is Eddie. My parents named me after an old French rock singer called Eddie Mitchell."

I was stunned by his direct approach. Being Japanese, I didn't know how to say no, so I said yes.

Anyway, as you can imagine, Momo has long since gone back to Japan. She left me in care of Takahashi-san from the Japanese

Embassy. My mother was really worried, and wanted to come over to be with me. But eventually, she was reassured by the care of the Embassy. Also, she said that a French friend of hers, Jean, would visit me. She must be one of my mother's French girlfriends.

Hiddey

My name is Hiddey. I am doing a masters degree in economics at UGW in Tokyo. I am researching certain aspects of Japan's never-ending economic crisis. It's amazing what a mess our government has made of our country. But who is really responsible?

For a number of years, my father was a professor in the US, at New York University. Today, he is also at the UGW where he teaches sociology. Thanks to our time in the US, I speak fairly good English. My English is not perfect, I know, but it's not bad. It's very much better than all my friends. I have heard that Japan's English language capacity is the worst in Asia, even worse than in North Korea!

I can't understand why our English is so bad. The science of language instruction is pretty straight forward, everyone teaches languages these days. It's amazing how well the young Koreans and Chinese speak English. At Japanese universities, even the English professors don't speak English. They just explain English grammar using the Japanese language.

Anyway, thanks to my English language skills, I was hired as a research assistant at a small sociology research institute called the Japan Institute for Contemporary Society (JINCS). This helps cover my living expenses (I also have a free computer!). Because this institute has several American and other Asian researchers, my English language skills were considered even more important than my statistical and computing skills. Foreigners don't speak Japanese.

In fact, lots of young foreign students are learning Chinese, but no-one learns Japanese these days.

JINCS is a pretty strange place. Most of us have no work to do most of the time. We just sit there. This is the Japanese style. We sit there and count the minutes. If a big boss walks through our work area, I motion to shuffle some paper. I keep my desk a bit untidy, as this gives the impression that I am doing something.

I surf on the Internet quite a bit. I have mastered the art of showing the World Bank website on my screen when someone walks past. I do a quick flick with the mouse to switch from the other junk that I read, and games that I play. Unfortunately, access has been blocked to most sexy websites. I say most, because there are always new sites popping up, which are not yet blocked and which I manage to find.

JINCS has two branches. One looks at Japanese society, and the other looks at the societies of emerging Asia. I am not sure how effective we are. We have lots of conferences, lots of speeches. My bosses love making speeches. But nothing much ever gets published. And there are no new ideas, as far as I can see.

It's very frustrating being a young researcher like me. I have lots of ideas about how to modernize Japanese society, but we are not allowed to express our views. No-one is interested.

The management of JINCS is very, very bureaucratic. Our older female colleagues are always quoting rules about what we should and should not do. But there is no rule book which makes anything clear. Nevertheless, these old ladies know mountains of "rules".

We call these old ladies "otsubone-sama". I don't know how to translate that into English, but it is something like old battle-axe. They really rule the roost!

The higher level managers only have one way of doing everything. It has usually been approved by the otsubone-samas. We are not allowed to experiment with new ideas. We might make a mistake! Heaven forbid! That would be the end of our careers.

I see on the Internet that young people elsewhere in Asia are encouraged to discuss and debate economic and social issues. Other Asian governments are managing fairly well.

When I started my masters degree, I was so excited. I wanted to change the world. I guess I was influenced a lot by my time in America. Also, my supervisor is a distinguished Japanese professor. But I must say that he does not care about me. He just wants to use me as a research assistant for his own work. One time I wrote a great paper all by myself, and he put his name on it as a co-author.

As soon as I get my masters degree, I will leave this country. Nowhere is perfect, but universities in the US are more dynamic. They dominate lists of the world's best universities. And they seem to be trying to solve their country's problems.

Americans might be crazy. But they are not lazy and blasé like many Japanese professors.

Mimi

Eddie suggested that we meet at the top of rue Sainte-Anne. He said that this is the heart of the Japanese district in Paris. I read that Sainte-Anne was the mother of the Virgin Mary, who in turn was the mother of Jesus. I still have at least one thing in common with Mary, but I am not so sure how long this might last in Paris.

Eddie arrived about five minutes late. Apparently the French are always late. Being Japanese, I was of course ten minutes early.

When he arrived he kissed me on both cheeks. "You know Mimi, the custom in France is two kisses in Paris, three in the country and four in Marseilles."

"Thank God he doesn't come from Marseille", I said to myself. As you know, we Japanese don't kiss at all. We don't even touch, just a bow.

At first, I was disgusted by the kiss. He had a smelly breath, I guess from the traditional French cigarettes that he smoked. But as his lip saliva slowly dried on my cheeks I had goose bumps all over again. More than that, my breast nipples went all hard. I was hoping that he would not notice. But even with my small Japanese breasts, you could now see a firm nipple outline on my teeshirt.

He led the way, as we walked off. He pulled me close to him, and my breast grazed his chest. He now knows for sure that I am excited. How will I regain my composure?

In fact, it wasn't too hard to regain my composure. He talks all the time, non-stop.

"I will take you to the best ramen restaurant in rue Sainte Anne", Eddie assured me. He explained all the different types of ramen. Had he forgoton that I am Japanese? When we sat down in the restaurant, he explained the whole menu, and ordered for me. I have seen this in French movies -- the cocky French man selling himself to a lady. He tries to impress her with all of his knowledge and sophistication. Japanese men are not like that at all. They don't even know how to talk.

Eddie then got talking about politics.

"France needed a President with energy and vision, so we voted for Sarkozy, but he turned out to be a nervous loose canon", according to Eddie. "Germany's Chancellor Merkel is more solid and reliable. Her problem is that she is too conservative, stodgy and boring".

"The problem of the European Union", he continued, "is that there are now too many members. The euro doesn't work. Those sneaky British were wise to stay out. They can play lone ranger, and get away with it."

"I really like President Obama", he insisted, "but America is the new evil empire, trying to control the world, and undermine any political competitor. President Obama cannot control the Congress or even the CIA or FBI. It's all now been confirmed by Wikileaks."

I was amazed at his political knowledge, and especially his passionately held opinions. He would be good at debating. In Japan we don't discuss politics. We don't even study it properly. Since most of our exams are based on multiple-choice questions, we learn things by heart to be able to tick the right box.

I felt embarrassed that I could not contribute to the conversation. But Eddie didn't seem to mind.

To show that I was interested in something, I said:

"Eddie, I don't know much about politics, but I do love art, especially Monet's paintings. Do you know the Musee Marmottan?"

"No problem, Mimi," Eddie replied, "I will take you there right after lunch."

So we took the metro from Palais Royal to La Muette, the closest metro to the Musee Marmottan. We had a quick change at the station Franklin D. Rooseveldt, and in no time at all we got off the metro at La Muette. The Paris metro stinks. It is so dirty. And many of the people who take it are dirty too. But it is full of life. Some stations had singers or musicians. And sometimes a musician would get on the train, play a song, pass his hat around for money, and then get off. The Paris underground train system is really an underworld full of life.

The shops, cafes and restaurants around La Muette are so classy, quite different from what I had seen before. This must be the real France.

We walked past a sign pointing to the OECD. I think that means the Organisation for Economic Cooperation and Development. Even though the name sounds important, I am not sure what it does. I think that is where Princess Masako's father was once Japanese ambassador.

Then we crossed a beautiful garden. It looked so French, I was so happy to be there. And when we entered the Musee Marmottan, "oh la la". That's a French expression that Eddie taught me. The museum is just so beautiful. Beautiful old French furniture and decorations. I could not believe it. There were quite a few other Japanese tourists there. We all go to the same places, you know.

Eddie is such a leader. He took me straight down to the underground floor where all the Monet paintings are kept. I love men like that, who take care of a lady. I've seen that in those old Cary Grant movies.

Those paintings are so beautiful. Each one is so wonderful and subtle. Each one is a dream world with water lilies floating and bending in different directions, against a dreamy, cloudy background. Sometimes I would close my eyes and then fantasize about floating among the water lilies. I could not speak of this with Eddie.

We sat down in the middle of the room and just gazed at the paintings. It seemed like hours. And it may well have been more than an hour that we sat there. As he explained each painting to me, Eddie would put his arm around my shoulders. It was not really sexy, but "oh so sensual". For some strange reason, I did not feel ill at ease. Like in Naoshima, these Monet paintings transported me to another world. And it seems that Eddie was there to transport me even further.

Eddie lives in the rue d'Auteuil. He suggested that we walk in the direction of his apartment because we would pass by the Le Corbusier Foundation. Like most Japanese people, I love Le Corbusier's architecture. By the time we reached the front gate, it was already closed. From the outside, I could easily admire the building and see some of the furniture inside. I want to go back.

So we walked off. By this time, he was holding me tightly. I didn't know whether I should worry or not. We stopped in at a café called Le Fetiche for a drink. With a name like that, I imagined some sort of sex shop. But no, it was just another café.

And then he broke the big news to me.

"Mimi, I have just been offered a one semester teaching job at the University of Great Wisdom in Tokyo. In fact, I am due to depart for Tokyo in two weeks' time. We could be together in Tokyo!"

Miyuki

Hi, I'm Miyuki back again. I've just had coffee again with Masa, the man who molested me in the metro.

He was delirious. He was raving on about his daughter Mimi who went to Paris against his orders and who wound up in hospital. Mimi is his last hope. His son committed suicide, and Mimi is his only remaining child. He loves her dearly and wants her to succeed in her career and her life. She is the only thing that he lives for, especially now that he barely talks with his wife.

He wanted her to study law at Tokyo University. That is the sure way to get a good job in Japan, be it in a government ministry or a large company. Even if law might have little practical value in your job, it is the prestige that counts. That's how it works in Japan. You get a job based on the prestige of your university and course. And a good job means status and security, everything that a Japanese person wants.

But Mimi insisted on studying sociology at the UGW. Since they have a good international program, it is a good way to learn English and meet international kids. But it is no way to get a good job in Japan. Mimi just wouldn't listen to him.

Masa kept raving on. "Life is much tougher now than when I was a kid. Despite being a woman, 30 or 40 years ago Mimi could have landed a job in a large enterprise like Toyota, Panasonic or Sony.

She would already be married. I could have arranged her marriage through friends of mine. Or, she could have met someone at the office. That's how we do it in Japan. Sure, she would leave work after having a child, but she would be married."

"But now stupid Mimi is working at Doutor serving coffee. What use was it to earn a masters degree in sociology. She's living comfortably in my house. My wife doesn't help by cooking her meals, washing her clothes, and giving her pocket money."

"Mimi just doesn't realize all we did after the war to provide for her life. I studied hard at university, I did law at Tokyo University, and got a good job in a Japanese bank. Those were the days. Japan recovered amazingly from the destruction of World War 2. I remember studying that by the early 1950s our economy had recovered to our pre-war level. Sure, the Americans helped us with all those military bases protecting us against communism. Its open markets allowed our enterprises to export everything under the sun."

"I remember when we hosted the 1964 Olympic Games, a first for Asia. We were so proud, even though a Dutch boy beat a Japanese boy to win the judo gold medal. In the same year, Japan became a member of the international rich man's club, the Organisation for Economic Cooperation and Development."

"Then we created the Asian Development Bank in 1966. We were no longer an aid recipient. We had made it. We were now going to lead Asia, like we tried to do before the war. Those countries that we invaded like China, Korea and Taiwan would look up to us again. We would provide them with assistance. And we would show them how it's done. Because quite frankly, it was our own Japanese model that was the secret of our success – a close partnership between government, business and finance. It's different from the American cowboy approach to capitalism."

"We didn't have to worry too much about democracy. Our government and business provided our citizens with jobs, lifetime employment, stability and safety. This is the Japanese model. All of our Asian friends would respect our model, especially since already by 1968 we overtook West Germany to become the world second largest economy. Japan had made it! We were by then just like a Western country, something it had always dreamed since the opening of the Meiji Restoration."

"Then we thought we could be number one, that we could overtake America. An American intellectual called Ezra Vogel even wrote a book called 'Japan as Number One'. But it all went to our head, and ended up in crisis. Our banks went crazy, lending money willy-nilly to any project, based on our system of personal relations. Our enterprises made all sorts of silly investments. We were in a bubble. And rather than pushing our economy to give up manufacturing and become a services dynamo, the government burst the bubble, and left us in a mess."

"We had a period of false optimism in the first part of the new millennium under Prime Minister Koizumi. But with the global financial crisis, we are now back in crisis."

"This is the world in which poor Mimi finds herself. Big corporations and government will not give you a job unless you have been to a top university, like Tokyo University, or unless you have a special skill like engineering. A Masters' degree in sociology from the UGW will not get you anywhere. And once you have missed the first intake to a company or government ministry, there is no second chance in Japan. You have missed the boat. This is not America, a land of endless opportunity."

I felt so sorry for Masa.

Mimi

Hi, I'm Mimi, back again. Eddie and I decided to stay on at the Fetiche café and have dinner.

I ordered confit de canard. I thought that after my bad experience in the Air France flight over here, I should give it another try. I was not disappointed this time. It is a sort of duck preserved in fat, and then crispy fried and served with sliced potatoes cooked in garlic oil. It was so delicious.

Eddie ordered steak tartare. This is raw minced beef mixed up with herbs and spices. He is always so French wanting to demonstrate his virility and carnivorous nature.

You won't believe it, but Eddie had never spoken to me about his career (he is actually an economist). You know, he always leads, or should I say, dominates the conversation. I can't get a word in edgeways. So he started to tell me all about his job at the UGW.

Japanese universities are now trying to jump on the bandwagon of the international higher education market. As everyone knows, those English speaking countries like the United States, United Kingdom and Australia attract lots of foreign students. It's a good source of revenues for the universities. For the United States, it's also a way to brainwash young students, especially from developing countries, with American values. The French have always done this too as they try to export the French language and culture to the rest of the world.

The latest development is China, which is attracting lots of young kids wishing to learn Chinese. So Japan feels once again left behind. One problem, most kids want their international education in the English language, and Japan has very few professors who can speak good English. So even a French man like Eddie can land a teaching job in Japan.

But Eddie told me his real motivation is his passion for manga, anime and other forms of contemporary Japanese culture. I hadn't realized but France is a land of manga mania. In fact, it is the world's second manga capital after Japan, perhaps because France always had a well-developed cartoon market. Even I had read Asterix and Tintin when I was a kid at the library of the Institut Franco-Japanais in Yokohama.

Eddie went on and on about manga, sushi and Japan. I am getting used to him now. As we were talking, I didn't notice how much we were drinking until he ordered a second bottle of Gevrey Chambertin, his favourite wine. It was red of course. The French always drink red wine. I had never drunk so much in all my life. But it was wonderful. I wasn't sure what was the most intoxicating, the wine or Eddie's charms.

As we left the restaurant, he held me tight. He kissed me all over my face, around my neck and down my back. I thought that I didn't like kissing, but this was different. I lost all sense of self control. He took me back to his apartment block, carried me up the stairs and placed me in his bed. I dozed off.

Then suddenly I awoke to the most magical music. It was a floating, dreamy music, without any definite structure or form. It actually sounded rather Asian, Chinese I thought. Then Eddie's mouth and hands swam all over my body. It was just like my fantasy of the water lilies. And when his tongue caressed my "schweetu-spotto", I began screaming and must have lost consciousness once again.

I woke up in the middle of the night to the rain dropping on the skylight window. It was so wonderful. I didn't know what to do, so I just snuggled up to him. The safest thing was not to think at all. Strangely, I didn't feel any pain at all. Japanese girls usually believe that sex will be painful. May be there is a special French technique that Eddie knows.

As I lay in bed I slowly awoke. I thought that I could smell coffee and croissants. Sure enough, with his typical enthusiasm, Eddie was preparing breakfast in the kitchen below. And that strange music was playing again.

So I put on one of Eddie's kimonos – he has a dozen of them – and went downstairs. I felt embarrassed. I think that I became a woman last night. Seeing him in the light of day was so awkward. But there he was, brimming with typical French self confidence, and making the coffee. He gave me a quick kiss and asked me how much sugar I take, and whether I wanted jam with my croissant. It seemed just like a normal morning to him. It was very, very far from normal to me.

He told me that he had to go to work, that I was welcome to stay the day, and that I should be there to meet him in the evening. He scoffed down his coffee, and without any further ado, he was off and away.

So after eating my breakfast, I went back up to bed. I quickly fell asleep. When I awoke, I was crying, sweating and all confused. What had happened? What did I do? But then I said to myself, "it's done".

I went downstairs again, and went looking for the CD of Asian music. I couldn't believe it. It was the music of a 20th century Japanese composer, Takemitsu Toru. I must confess that I had never heard of him. The music that we listened to last night and this morning was called "I Hear the Water Dreaming", a piece for flute and orchestra. It was so exquisite that I listened to it again. I took a peek inside Eddie's CD cabinet and saw that he had dozens of CDs by Takemitsu. As I walked around the apartment, I noticed Japanese paintings and porcelain, and then I entered a room full of manga.

I was overcome by it all. I needed to go outside and take some fresh air.

Hiddey

It's Hiddey back with you. My stay at JINCS is becoming interesting. I have always believed that to understand politics and government policy, you must understand society. And to understand society, you must see how people work together. And this is what I can see here.

Back before the bubble economy, Japanese business and government were idealized by the West. But I don't think that too many Western people looked closely at how we really work. Anyway, Japanese society and people are impenetrable for Westerners.

I also get the impression that those Westerners who are working at our institute are free-riding on the system. They all seem to be in slow motion, watching their Japanese colleagues run around in circles. The other day, Jack, who is always making jokes, groaned out loud in front of me, "it's terrible, my efficiency has fallen to Japanese levels". I could not believe it. How could he be so brazen? Even if that's true, he should not say it.

Since he is a nice sort of avuncular fellow, I went into his office and talked with him. He suddenly looked unhappy. He confessed to me that he joined JINCS about thirty years ago when he realized that the Japanese needed three times as many office workers as Western companies for doing the same job. "I realized that I would have a much easier life than in America. One problem, though. After being in a Japanese organization for some 30 years, my own level of efficiency has slipped way back too." Here is Jack's story.

He has gone native. He deeply regrets his decision to work and live in Japan. Sure, life is very comfortable and pleasant. But there is no electricity and dynamism. Creative workers like researchers are always blocked by the bureaucrats. Young people are crushed by older people and the seniority system. Women are never given a fair chance. And Westerners are never trusted by their Japanese colleagues, and always kept out of the loop. They will never trust what Westerners say. They will always double check with another Japanese. They always imagine that foreigners are ripping off their systems, so they never share all our information with them.

They use Westerners when they need them. If they need contacts with Western companies, research institutes or universities, the Westerner will always take the lead. Even then, the Westerner must always hold himself back and give the limelight to the Japanese bosses. Sometimes Japanese organizations want to give the impression of being international, so they wheel out a few Westerners for show. But fundamentally, Japanese organizations are always make a split between the Japanese and the gaijin, the foreigner. And most gaijin in Japanese organizations end up with their spirits crushed. You see them with their hunched backs and nervous twitches.

But they are comfortable, and no-one would ever fire a Westerner. The Japanese suffer from a mixture of superiority and inferiority complexes, which blocks any action that they might contemplate towards a Westerner.

"Do these foreigners in Japan have anything in common?", I asked him.

"Yes", he replied, "we all have Japanese wives who insist on living in Japan. May be we are all a bit weak willed, and are trapped by their charms and cannot escape. It's a kinda easy life. The only thing the wives request is that we hand over our pay once a month, in return for the freedom to spend our monthly pocket money. My wife actually holds on to my credit card. Sometimes I think that she has made a little boy out of me."

"But Hiddey, if you want to understand Japanese governance, just take a look at our office here at JINCS. It is in the smallest of institutions that you can really see the processes of human organization and interaction. Just look at all these bureaucrats. They are running round in circles, checking, double-checking, doing anything to avoid responsibility. These bureaucrats invent terrible systems for multiple signatures and approvals. Can you imagine physical signatures and stamps in today's computerized world?"

"It is really sad. In systems which are based on blindly following rules, trust between colleagues never develops. It is all about process, process, process, with everyone is watching each other to see if they follow the rules correctly. Suspicion reigns. What's more there are all sorts of invisible rules that must be followed. Because they have been doing something in a certain way for twenty years, they must keep doing it that way. If someone asks why a certain thing is done in a certain way, they can defend themselves by saying that it has always been done that way."

"One of the worst things are the Japanese 'confessionals'. As you know, when a Japanese staff member is late by 5 or 10 minutes, they must send their colleagues an email apology. This is simply childish. We gaijin do not have to make these silly apologies. When someone makes a tiny little mistake, they must also write an 'I'm sorry message' to the head of administration and his other colleagues. In return, you receive a message saying that you are forgiven, but that it should never happen again. Even we Westerners have to submit ourselves to such nonsense. Every week or two, I find that I have transgressed some silly little rule, and must beg for forgiveness and understanding. Confessionals are designed to humiliate Japanese into obedience and submission. But the Japanese spend so much time saying sorry that the word no longer has any real meaning."

"These office rules are never clear and explicit. They are managed by the office's otsubone-sama, the old battle-axe over there in the corner. You can tell her importance by the position of her desk, and all the filing cabinets that surround her. There is no electronic filing here, the old ladies don't know how to use computers very well. The otsubone-sama wields immense authority over all the younger office ladies, and even over the male bosses who see in otusbone-sama the wrath of their mother, and obey instantly."

"Another thing which is not always visible on the outside is the complex management and social hierarchies, where respect and obedience must be shown to all superiors, although the exact nature of the hierarchy may not be clear. People talk about Confucianism in Japan, but it is very little present. Japan has always been fundamentally a feudal and militaristic society. You see it everywhere."

"Since I have been in Japan, I have thought a lot about democracy, and what it really means. Americans preach democracy all the time, you know. I think that the essence of democracy is not elections, nor the separation of powers between the executive, legislative and judicial branches of government. The essence of democracy is that sovereignty resides with the people, and that government is elected to serve the people. In Japan, the people have no sense of being in control of their country or destiny. They are always sitting there waiting for orders to follow. I don't that we will ever see democracy in Japan in my lifetime, real democracy that is."

"Of course, the Japanese are not stupid. And they can be efficient in some areas. No Westerner could cut sushi with the accuracy and precision of a Japanese sushi-man. No Western could serve a coffee as quickly."

"Other parts of the service sector, like banks, are almost as bureaucratic and inefficient as government bureaucrats. And you watch, when the big boss wants something from the Japanese office worker, they flood him with material, rather than focusing on the essential. They get higher marks for effort than for results, and they avoid the risk of punishment from misdirected precision."

"I recently met a certain Kondo-san at a bar who said 'I am an electrical engineer. I like making things.' This is the real spirit of Japan, the country that invented the Walkman and has flooded world markets with all sorts of products and gadgets for decades."

"But even here, the Japanese are best at copying something from someone else, then perfecting it and adapting it slightly. But don't wait for the big idea or major break through. The Japanese are experts at what they call 'incremental innovation', but this is because they are too afraid to attempt a bold initiative."

"The question that Japan has to face up to whether this system can last. Japan has the world's best blue collar workers and some of the world's worst managers. It cannot go on like this. The world has changed. Japan has not kept pace. And it is now being overtaken by Korea, Taiwan and China."

I was just flabbergasted after hearing all of this. "But it does somehow ring true", I said to myself.

Mimi

As I was leaving Eddie's apartment, I noticed a book entitled "le wabi-sabi japonais", and took it with me.

I have vaguely heard of this wabi-sabi, but I am not really sure what it is. As I walked onto the sidewalk, there was a cool breeze drifting down rue d'Auteuil, which helped me settle down a little. But walking into the western sun, I could not quite see clearly, and was not sure where I was going.

Next thing, I stumbled upon the café where we had dinner last night, le Fetiche. I went in, and ordered a café crème. In Tokyo, no-one but no-one talks in cafes and there is certainly no familiarity between the servers and the customers. So I was taken aback when the servers recognized and greeted me warmly. They even kissed me, 'la petite japonaise'. I was so embarrassed. They chatted and flirted, quite like Eddie does. I must confess that I actually enjoyed their human warmth.

Eventually they left me in peace, and I tried to read 'le wabi-sabi japonais'. I had great difficulty understanding. It was not so much the French language, but the vague and abstract descriptions.

Someone called Leonard Koren describes wabi-sabi as as a beauty that is 'imperfect, impermanent, and incomplete'. It involves aesthetic features like asymmetry, asperity, simplicity, modesty, intimacy, and the suggestion of natural processes. Someone else called Andrew

Juniper claims, 'if an object or expression can bring about, within us, a sense of serene melancholy and a spiritual longing, then that object could be said to be wabi-sabi'. The book even quotes architect, Tadao Ando, 'wabi-sabi is the Japanese art of finding beauty in imperfection and profundity in nature, of accepting the natural cycle of growth, decay, and death'. Ando designed the Chichu Art Museum on Naoshima which houses the beautiful Monet water lily paintings.

Since I didn't really understand what all this meant, I decided to go to an Internet café and look up wabi-sabi in Japanese. It might be easier if I were in Japan, I could simply look up wabi-sabi on my mobile phone. But Japanese mobile phones don't work outside the country. It's so strange.

More and more Japanese technology is being invented for the local market in isolation from the rest of the world. I don't understand. The rest of the world is coming together through the use of common technological standards, and we are drifting away and isolating ourselves. I heard someone call this the Galapagos Syndrome. Japan is becoming like the Galapagos Islands with its weird and unique fauna and flora. How will we ever compete with other countries or even understand other countries if we keep going on long this?

I know that my father criticizes me for studying sociology, but it is through studying the social sciences that you can actually begin to understand the world. Studying technical subjects like law or engineering or even economics just pushes you down into a narrow technical hole. And what's more, Japanese technical experts usually don't speak English and have no idea what their counterparts in other countries are doing.

Anyway, I found a nice little Internet café, which happened to be just next to a Chinese massage parlor. The Chinese massage girls were walking in the street looking for customers. They are so entrepreneurial. The employee of the Internet café was very friendly, he helped me log on and offered me a coffee. French men are often very nice with ladies, or with me at least.

On the Japanese language websites I found more information on wabi-sabi. Some examples are rustic and simple pottery, fading autumn leaves, ageing bare wood, Zen music, Japanese gardens, and bonsai. It sounds so beautiful and peaceful.

I found another quote from Tadao Ando, 'Wabi-sabi is flea markets, not warehouse stores; aged wood, not Pergo; rice paper, not glass. It celebrates cracks and crevices and all the other marks that time, weather, and loving use leave behind. It reminds us that we are all but transient beings on this planet-that our bodies as well as the material world around us are in the process of returning to the dust from which we came. Through wabi-sabi, we learn to embrace liver spots, rust, and frayed edges, and the march of time they represent.'

Reading through all this, I found myself dreaming of Japan, with its old temples, gardens and decorative objects. As I wandered off around the back streets of Auteuil, I thought that I would look for the Le Corbusier Foundation again. I would love to visit it.

As I walked, it was strange, I felt an atmosphere of wabi-sabi. Auteuil has so many old buildings which show the cracks and chips of old age. Some buildings may not have been renovated for a hundred years. Some streets have cobble stone. I was overcome by the rustic charm. And although the people are well dressed, many of them looked slightly shabby. They looked a bit like artists.

It made me think back to Japan. Although you can find elements of wabi-sabi in Japan, you really have to look hard. May be it's because we have lost so many of our old buildings in earthquakes like the Great Kanto Earthquake of 1923 which totally flattened Tokyo. Then there was World War 2 which again demolished much of our country.

But quite honestly, I think that while we may like to idealize the aesthetics of wabi-sabi, it does not reflect our true nature. We do not rejoice in imperfection and incompleteness. We are a very meticulous and finicky people, obsessed with cleanliness and details. I have never seen a Japanese person get excited about a dying lotus or peony flower. In fact, much of Tokyo is quite simply gaudy and crass, especially the ubiquitous Pachinko parlors. And the most distinctive feature of our cities is the coffee shops like Doutor and Starbucks which are everywhere. It is somehow sad that the Japanese wabi-sabi aesthetic seems to be more appreciated by foreigners like Eddie than by ourselves.

As I was wandering the backstreets of Auteuil, I was in a trance. The whole area is so charming with old buildings, and trees and cafes everywhere. In fact, I felt it all seemed so wabi-sabi. I suddenly happened upon the Le Corbusier Foundation. I was not disappointed. Inside the main building of the Foundation, I was transfixed by the beautiful lines of the architecture. What captured my attention most was the 'long chair'. Le Corbusier apparently once said: 'Chairs are architecture, sofas are bourgeois.' That's so beautiful.

There were other things that also surprised me. I discovered that Le Corbusier was Swiss, not French. It's amazing how many famous French people are not actually French. What's more, Le Corbusier's real name is Charles-Édouard Jeanneret. Just like Stendhal, Le Corbusier adopted a name. France has so many famous people. But just like wabi-sabi, they're all dead now. I wonder if there are any famous people in France today.

Sandy

Hi, I'm Sandy back again. You may not believe it, but between Doutor and the massages, I actually do have time for my studies.

My favorite subject at university is international migration. Our nickname for our professor is "Professor Worry Potter" – sounds like Harry Potter! When we ask him a question, he suddenly has a worried look on his face. And then his voice is so boring that even he sometimes potters off to sleep during his own lectures. But he's a nice guy as far as professors go.

I like international migration because it always reminds me that humankind is one race, that we are one people. I firmly believe that. True, cultural diversity is deep. It is the product of the first great divergence in the history of humankind. From our beginnings in East Africa, perhaps 50,000 years ago, we migrated across the globe and settled in communities in a vast array of climes and landscapes. But now thanks to globalization, we are coming back together as one humankind. Deep down, we are all migrants from somewhere.

Through the course of history, China has seen many waves of migration and many dynasties come and go. We have experienced almost constant contact with other cultures. We were even invaded by peoples like the Mongols and Manchurians. But our culture is so wonderful and strong that all sorts of people have been absorbed into China. Also, we have radiated Chinese culture out to all of our neighboring countries. We are a continental people, with a big vision of the world, a bit like the Americans I feel.

The Japanese are very different, they are an island people sitting on the edge of universe, on the periphery of the Chinese world. They seem to have a deep sense of paranoia vis-à-vis the rest of the world which they think is unsympathetic and even hostile to Japan.

It is also a country which is schizophrenic. It left Asia to join the West, and now it's having difficulty finding a natural place in a resurgent Asia. Japan has been greatly influenced by Chinese culture, even though the Japanese have difficulty accepting that. Their historic dependence on Chinese culture has contributed to their irrationality and xenophobia. It makes them feel insecure, vulnerable and helpless.

Because of their isolation, they came to believe that they were somehow unique and special. Even today, they seem to delight in being different from others – to such a point that the best way to make a Japanese person happy is to tell them that you don't like sushi!

It's these attitudes that underlie their closed attitudes towards migration. Membership of the Japanese tribe is a question of blood. Japanese nationality is based on jus sanguinis.

Japan has however been gradually opening up a little to migration. But it has not been a happy experience. The Japanese government has been trying to encourage the entry of skilled migrants, but not so many are interested. The prospect of being a gaijin in a Japanese company, and imposing Japanese life on a Western family is not very attractive. There has been a dramatic increase in unskilled foreign workers, especially from China and other Asian countries, but many of these people are illegal immigrants. The poor girls usually end up working in bars, massage parlors or even worse, while the guys work in construction and other services industries where Japanese workers do not like to work -- Japan's 3K jobs, kiken (dangerous), kitsui (difficult) or kitanai (dirty).

The Japanese government loves ambiguity. It knows that there are many illegal migrants here. It knows that their country needs them in all sorts of occupations, including as elderly care workers and nurses. Japan needs migrants above all to put some entrepreneurial spark in its economy. Migrants are far more entrepreneurial than local populations, because they are hungry to succeed. And Chinese migrants are the most entrepreneurial of all. We make all sorts of business, and boost trade with our home land, which is already Japan's most important trading partner.

But I think that the Japanese are most afraid of all of our entrepreneurial abilities, because they are so conservative and risk averse. They fear that we might take them over. The Japanese people are even blaming Chinese immigrants for the increasing petty crime like shoplifting, pick-pocketing and burglary. In reality, as there are more and more homeless and poor Japanese people, they are resorting to crime out of desperation. The most tragic cases are old people who go shoplifting. Some one-quarter of all shop-lifting is done by old people who are poor, bored or lonely.

So the Japanese government provides no help or support whatsoever to these poor migrants. Why? One day the Japanese government may wish to get rid of these migrants, for some unforeseeable reason. And if they are still illegal, it's very easy to just throw them out on a one-way air ticket. Not nice!

A few of my Chinese friends and I are planning to create a migrant support organization to help these poor migrants. We can help migrants with everyday life issues they have to battle with. They need help desperately. Many of them are poor simple people from villages. Those Japanese bureaucrats don't like non-governmental organizations. They prefer to exercise absolute power. But they can't stop us from setting up our organization any more. No-one respects Japanese bureaucrats these days.

Mimi

Eddie and I were caressing each other at that moment of half-sleep just before waking up. We had become so close, perhaps deeply in love.

All of a sudden, Eddie sits up and says:

"Today's the day Mimi, I will take you to see Monet's house and garden at Giverny. The weather is beautiful and I am sure that the water lilies will look wonderful."

Eddie ran down stairs and prepared breakfast, coffee and croissants. "What a leader, I love him so much", I said to myself. I had by now forgoton all about natto and green tea, my typical breakfast in Tokyo.

Giverny is not much more than an hour's drive from Auteuil, so off we set in Eddie's old Jaguar. It had so much class, leather seats and wooden dash board. And he was quite a sight to see behind the steering wheel, a real show-off. But he was cute too.

Barely fifteen minutes out of Paris, Eddie's Jaguar came to a halt. He told me that Jaguars have a terrible reputation for reliability. Their complex electronic systems always break down.

Eddie had to call the Jaguar garage. They didn't make it out to the broken down car until after lunch. It took ages to fix the broken electronic system. In the end, they had to deactivate the automatic seat belts.

By now, it was mid-afternoon. Should we still go on to Giverny?

"Let's go", said Eddie, "we can find a nice little country hotel and stay overnight. You will see Mimi, the food in the French countryside is much better and cheaper. They always use fresh ingredients from the local area."

We made good progress and arrived at Giverny about seven o'clock in the evening. Even though Monet's house and garden were closed, we went over to have a look around. We noticed lots of bushes behind the water lily ponds, and so we went around and had a look. We walked our way around to a little stream that made a border between Monet's gardens and the bush. There was a small barbed wire fence that was designed to prevent access, but it had obviously been broken by other trespassers.

I don't know what came over me, but before Eddie could say anything, I had climbed through the barbed wire fence and crossed the stream, dancing my way across the rocks. It looked so much fun that Eddie just followed, even though he is not nearly as agile as me. We started tiptoeing through the garden.

"It is so beautiful, much better than I ever imagined", I exclaimed. We went all around the garden. There was not a soul in sight. Suddenly, we saw someone. It looked like another Japanese tourist. That person then scurried away in fright. "She obviously broke in like us", I whispered.

The garden was beautiful. The early evening summer weather was balmy. I was under the spell of the beautiful lily ponds, with lilies floating around almost imperceptibly and the light glistening through the willow trees. Eddie and I wandered off in different directions. Under the spell of this wondrous beauty, and unconscious of what I was doing, I took off all of my clothes and waded into one of the water lily ponds. I began floating on my back, making small strokes to keep a slight movement. The water lilies would glide over my body. I was in extasy.

A few ducks were also gliding gracefully on the surface of the lily pond, making their way through the floating water lilies. Then, all of a sudden, one duck glided into me, straight into my schweetu-spotto and obviously excited by the physical contact, the duck ruffles around for a few moments.

It was all too much for me. I unleashed the loudest of screams as I climaxed.

Sacre bleu! Sartori! Confit de canard!

The duck, and in fact all the ducks in the pond, rushed away, and left the pond and then sat on the bank on the side of the lily pond. Eddie came running over. He hadn't noticed that I had entered the pond nude, and could not believe his eyes.

Before Eddie comprehend in the situation, and also before I had time to dress myself, two security guards appeared. They were in uniform and seemed to be carrying shot guns. These French country security guards obviously seem to mix hunting and security operations.

As I was hurriedly dressing myself, Eddie spoke with the security guards and tried to beg them for understanding.

"We are just tourists. Our car had broken down. We found an easy way into the gardens through the broken fence. And most of all, Mimi is a great admirer of Monet's painting and French culture in general."

The guards would hear nothing of it. We were arrested and escorted to the police station in Giverny. At this point, I broke down in tears and was virtually hysterical. I couldn't find my passport, and couldn't answer questions. Eddie handled the situation the best he could. But he seemed very troubled himself by my bizarre behavior.

He yelled at me, "how could this shy little Japanese girl suddenly undress herself and start swimming in Monet's lily pond?".

By the time we got back to Eddie's car, he had dismissed any idea of staying in the country.

"I have too many thoughts spinning around in my head. Are you really the sweet little Japanese girl that I imagined and had fallen in love with? Or are you capable of more unpredictable and embarrassing behavior? Do you even understand your own behavior?"

"You know, I am very open minded. I love the idea of a women with an erotic spirit. But getting arrested totally nude in Monet's lily pond is just too much."

As we started driving back, there was at first a deathly silence in the car …

Hiddey

I am still shaken by Jack's story about life in Japan I could sense that something was awry, but did not imagine that Jack could unload such a terrible story like that.

I really had noticed something kinda strange myself. People don't cooperate much in our office. The teams working on Japanese society and emerging Asian societies are at opposite ends of the floor of our building, and don't mix much together. Apparently, this occurs everywhere, although in Japan it seems endemic. We call it 'tatewari gyousei' meaning a vertically segmented administrative system.

There is a nice lady in our office who is a research assistant. She is very friendly by Japanese standards. Most of my colleagues don't talk much with each other. Her name is Chichiko. So I decided to try to speak with her. It might be interesting for my thesis on Japan's reform process. It might even be useful for developing my own survival capacities.

I should say that early the other morning, I was jogging past McDonald's and I thought that I saw Chichiko serving behind the counter. I could not believe my eyes. It was hard to be sure, because she was all dressed up in a McDonald's uniform.

I waited for Chichiko to go down for her daily coffee at Doutor, and then I followed her. I was standing behind her in the queue and then acted in a surprised way when she saw me. She asked me to join for coffee. She even treated me to coffee. I guess she took pity on me as a young student.

We started talking, just like that. I mentioned, a bit sneakily, that I go jogging every morning around Kagurasaka. She instantly responded that she works at McDonald's in the morning. She asked me to not mention this to our colleagues. Legally, we are not allowed to have a second job. Also, it would be humiliating for her to be seen at McDonald's. She is after all a research assistant with a Masters degree from the UGW. I mentioned to her that my father is a professor there.

She said that her day starts at McDonald's at 6.00. She serves the breakfast customers from 6.00 to 8.30. Now that we Japanese are getting poorer, McDonald's is capturing the breakfast market. They serve a breakfast "seto" for 200 yen, about $2.50. Chichiko's McDonald's shop is open 24 hours a day. People can sleep on their coffee. She told me that there is something about the flavor of McDonald's products. You get used to the taste. You want more. They're kinda addictive.

I asked her about the atmosphere at our research institute. She agreed that it was a pretty cold and uncooperative atmosphere. She told me that atmosphere at McDonald's is also kinda strange. They pride ourselves on rapid service -- the faster, the better. But she thinks that most of her colleagues behave like robots. They never smile.

She insisted that that did not stop her from smiling. She has always been a smiley person. She said that she has always been a valued staff member at McDonald's because she speaks English fluently. She can serve the foreign customers easily. Sometimes they are tourists. But there are also migrants -- from the Philippines, Indonesia and China. Japan has always been pretty closed to migrants, but there are more and more of them all the time. Chichiko didn't know how they get into our country, but they certainly are here. Anyway, they all speak English better than Japanese. And because they have little money, McDonald's is ideal for them.

Chichiko told me that she perfected her English when she was living in the US, upstate New York, actually. She loved the US. It is friendly, open and fun. But she had to come back to Tokyo for her family. Her father was sick. He still is. Modern medicine keeps these old people alive forever. Many get depressed and some even commit suicide. But most hang on forever and ever. That's why Japan has the world's highest life expectancy.

But Chichiko told me that her salary at the research institute is peanuts. That's why she needs to work at McDonald's. In the Japanese research system, it's the high level bureaucrats who get the good salaries. They are usually parachuted down from a government job, after retirement (in Japanese we call this 'amakudari', descent from heaven). It doesn't seem fair. But this is the way it is in Japan.

Although Chichiko is a research assistant, she virtually runs two of our research programs. She really loves her job. But what interests her most is how Asian societies are reacting to globalization and rapid economic development. And she loves drawing comparisons between Japan and other Asian countries. Her pet thesis is that although Japan's economy is the most advanced in Asia, Japan's society might be the most backward.

Japan is a male dominated society. Women are treated like second class citizens, and not given a chance. Child care facilities are not widely available which means that women are virtually forced to leave their jobs when they have a baby. This is one reason why Japanese are no longer so keen to have children and why the country's birthrate is plummeting. Japanese men rarely spend time with their families. They are always out drinking with their colleagues, and going to girly bars and massage parlors.

Elsewhere in Asia, in countries like the China, Indonesia, Philippines, and Thailand, women are given a much better chance. Even Asia's

Muslim countries treat their women better than Japan does. And then there is the gerontocracy, the old people who dominate our society and crush the hopes and aspirations of the young. Why can't young kids get a chance these days? Because the old men are blocking all the positions. They won't retire. They never retire. They always get parachuted into another job, usually ending up as a geriatric professor somewhere like UGW, stopping young professors from climbing the ladder.

Chichiko believes that the Japanese government should stop worrying about the economy, and start trying to fix the country's broken society.

Mimi

I did not know what to say to Eddie in the car going back. To be frank, I was in a state. I did not know what came over me when I swam into Monet's water lily pond. I was also astonished by the intensity of Eddie's reaction. But deep down I was worried, deeply worried that Eddie could sense that the duck had excited me more than he had. And I was also perplexed that I could be so excited by a duck. "Am I weird and perverse?" Like Eddie, I had so many things going around in my head.

After driving for about a quarter of an hour, Eddie broke the ice. He apologized for overreacting. Eddie slowly got his feelings off his chest:

"I can imagine how tempting it was to jump into Monet's water lily pond. The weather was so warm and balmy. The pond looked so beautiful with the water lilies floating."

"I was surprised that you should swim nude. It's not that I have anything against that. But I had never seen you be quite so spontaneous before. The possibility that someone else should see your beautiful body made me feel jealous. I love you much, and feel possessive. We Latin men are like that."

"I wouldn't say that I was jealous of the duck, but the whole scene of the duck swimming into you, and then your screaming was just so erotic. I did not know how I felt. I guess that I wish I were there with you."

"The whole scene reminded me of the Leda and the Swan motif from Greek mythology. Zeus came to Leda in the form of a swan who bore him two children, while at the same time she had two children to her husband, the King of Sparta."

"I am not really an expert in Greek mythology. But I came to learn of Leda and the Swan when I was studying Renaissance painting at the Louvre. At the time of the Renaissance, it was quite customary to paint a woman in the act of copulation with a swan rather than with a man. I was particularly struck by Leonardo da Vinci's painting of the subject showing a nude Leda who was cuddling the Swan, with the two sets of infant twins, and their huge broken egg-shells."

I was simply bamboozled by Eddie's explanation. The French are really so complicated, I thought. Everything in life is weighed down by heavy references to culture and history.

As I reflected on it, my thoughts wandered back to my sociological studies on high and low context cultures. I know that both French and Japanese have high context cultures, but we are still very, very different. Neither of us may need to be explicit when communicating among ourselves. Many things can be left unsaid. But our contexts are so different.

"You know, Eddie," I said, "we come from quite different cultures. True, we both come from very old cultures, with old traditions. We are both very proud peoples, and like to keep our independence from other countries. It is also true that we both come from elite-dominated societies which have given us rich cultural heritages."

"But we Japanese are taught to hide our feelings and emotions, and to never express of our real opinions, especially if they might offend other people. We always show respect to elders and superiors, and never question them."

"What's more, Japanese tend to be intuitive and emotional, not logical like you French people with your Cartesian logic. Our language is even like this as we have to pay great attention to all the social nuances necessary in addressing people of different social rank. This is far more important to us than logic or rationality. As our Nobel prize winning author Kenzaburo Oe has said vagueness is inherent in the Japanese language."

"I think that it is in part because of all this that we Japanese all feel under intense pressure. We are constantly pressurized to behave in certain ways, and to be careful, cautious, humble, modest and respectful. And I feel under so much pressure at certain times that sometimes I just snap. That's what happened when I arrived in Paris, and I ended up in the Hotel Dieu. And I think that's what happened at Monet's water lily pond."

Eddie held my hand very tenderly as he was driving. With every breath I took, I could feel my spirit being filled with his love. I had never felt that way before. No words were spoken during the rest of the trip. After arriving in Paris, we spent the evening in a deep passionate embrace. We couldn't let go of each other all night.

Miyuki

I was beginning to tire of Masa and his diatribes. But I could sense his great emotional fragility and was afraid to stop seeing him for fear of how he might react.

But once again, he started raving on.

"When I was working in the bank, in the good old times of the bubble economy, it was great. Sure, I no longer had any meaningful relationship with my wife. We hadn't made love since her pregnancy with Mimi. And the real rupture came when our son committed suicide. My wife blamed me for not caring for our son, and causing his depression. Since then, we have not really spoken."

"But I used to go out with my colleagues every evening, drinking and womanizing. It was great. Girls came from everywhere, Thailand, the Philippines, Taiwan and Korea. And they would do anything you want. My company had an enormous expense account which covered this. What I enjoyed most was the "no-pan shabu shabu" restaurants where the waitresses serving this Japanese hot pot did not wear panties. The real fun was trying to see under their dresses thanks to the mirrored floors -- always a challenge, but great fun."

"But times have changed. After many scandals reported in the press, lots of these bars have closed down. And as the bursting of the bubble economy hit our companies, the wild expense accounts dried up too. I have also heard that the government has been trying to crack down on human trafficking of all these girls from South East Asia. The American government, international organizations and human rights' NGOs have been putting pressure on the Japanese government to clean up our sex industry."

"They'll never clean it up properly. I've read that it could even account for 2 to 3 per cent of GDP, and be double the size of Japan's agricultural sector. And the yakuza, the Japanese mafia, have a stranglehold over this, and also have too many embarrassing things on many of our politicians. But still it is not the same."

"For me, all the fun has gone out of life. After the bubble burst, my bank found it self with the 'three excesses', debt, capacity and people. And I lost my job. Fortunately, one of my old batch mates ('dockey') could offer me a job in his company. My salary is much lower, and I don't have the same status or prestige. But at least I have job and income. I don't think that my wife is happy with my salary, but she doesn't complain and still gives for 50,000 yen monthly pocket money. She didn't even cut it when the current global financial crisis struck. Somehow, she seems to have lots of money."

"So, I go out drinking with my new colleagues. Then we sometimes go hostess bars and to lap-dancing clubs. But I am on a tight budget, and often have to borrow money from my colleagues near the end of the month."

"My company has been suffering badly since the Lehman shock of September 2008, and the change of government in September 2009. Exports crashed in 2009, and are only picking up slowly. And the Democratic Party of Japan government has provoked instability everywhere. The first Prime Minister Yukio Hatoyama decided to turn his back on the Americans and cosy up to the Chinese. How naïve? Then he promised to cut carbon emissions. We can't afford that. And then he caused so much confusion about the American bases in Okinawa that the only thing left to do was resign."

"Then we have Naoto Kan as Prime Minister. At least he is more decisive. But he makes the wrong decisions. He made an increase in consumption taxes the centerpiece of his campaign to be elected head of political party."

"Back in the good old days with the Liberal Democratic Party government, we used to work out everything with the bureaucrats, and the politicians would just rubber stamp the decisions. Sure, we still haven't really made it out of the post-bubble crisis. But we had a system that worked for our company. The new government doesn't understand reality, it will take them a long while to know how to govern. And the media does not help either, they don't really understand."

"Now like many companies, we are struggling under the weight of five obstacles – high yen, high taxes (the highest among the OECD countries), slow progress on free trade agreements, labor regulations, and environmental regulations to reduce carbon emissions. Like many Japanese companies, we are sitting on lots of savings. But from a business point of view, the only sensible thing to do is to move all of our production facilities offshore in China and Vietnam."

"I have volunteered to move overseas, but the company management think that I am too old. I will push them again. I would love to go overseas. That would get me away from my wife and Mimi. Our salaries overseas are much higher with lots of allowances."

By the end of this drivel, I told Masa that I had had enough. I don't want to see him ever again, if he was going to carry on raving like this all the time.

I liked him well enough, but he should start to take an interest in me. I don't think that he had ever been spoken to like this before, and seemed to not know how to react. As a typical Japanese man, saying sorry would not come easily to him. But he seemed to think about it.

"Miyuki, you know that you are the only woman in the world who I have ever been able to talk to. As a proud Japanese man, it is difficult for me to say sorry. Japanese men would never say sorry to a woman.

Can I invite you to a beautiful restaurant tomorrow evening. We can try to start again."

Mimi

It was only a few days before Eddie and I were due to fly off to Tokyo. I changed my ticket so that I could be on the same plane as Eddie. He let me use his frequent flyer card miles to get an upgrade to business class and sit next to him on the plane.

I thought that I must make the effort to meet with her mother's friend, Jean. When I telephoned, I was shocked to hear a beautiful male voice. I hadn't realized that Jean was French for John.

He suggested that we meet in front of a restaurant called "La Tour d'Argent". I looked this up in the dictionary and discovered that it meant "silver tower". I thought that it must be good. Indeed, it was very good.

Jean arrived a little late, like Eddie did at rue Sainte Anne. These French men are all the same. He looked about 60 years old, a good few years older than my mother. But he was very, very elegant and charming.

"You must be Mimi", he said, speaking English with a sexy French accent. He didn't know that I am more comfortable in French than in English. He lifted my right hand to his mouth and gave it the most delicate and slowest kiss I had ever experienced. I had goose bumps all over again.

As he escorted me up to the restaurant, I felt that I had been whisked away, literally swept off my feet. He had booked what seemed to be the best table in the restaurant. He gave me the seat overlooking Notre Dame Cathedral. That reminded me that I should go back to the Hotel Dieu to bid farewell to the doctors and nurses who took such good care of me.

Jean explained that we must order the duck. "Oh no, confit de canard", I exclaimed to herself. Perhaps sensing some reticence, Jean immediately launched into an insistent explanation, much like Eddie does.

Jean claimed that the origins of the famous duck of la Tour d'Argent date back to the reign of Philip IV of Spain, in 1650. Apparently, Spanish emigrants arrived on the coast of France, and captured and domesticated wild ducks which are the very ancestors of the duck we will eat today.

I noticed Wagyu marbled beef on the menue, but did not dare contradict Jean after his long and convoluted explanation. He strongly recommended that we share a duckling with orange sauce. We could start with some "Foie gras des Trois Empereurs". He concluded that we could not leave the restaurant without tasting the restaurant's ever so delicate crepes "Belle Epoque".

Then, even without consulting me, he ordered a bottle of Gevrey Chambertin and sparkling water. "That's exactly what Eddie ordered at le Fetiche", I said to myself, "these French men think that they are individualist, but they seem to suffer just as much as we Japanese do from social engineering".

With the meal ordering out of the way, I thought that we could sit back and talk. I was really keen to learn of his relationship with my mother. Like Eddie, he launched off onto a charming and witty tirade which was to leave me in a state of shock.

"You know", he said, "every time I come to Tokyo, I take your mother to la Tour d'Argent in the New Otani Hotel. It's her favorite

French restaurant in Tokyo. We always take a private salon so as not to be disturbed by any surprise visitors."

"In fact, Tokyo is the only other place in the world to have a la Tour d'Argent restaurant. It is really charming with its antique furniture. It really captures the atmosphere of the original la Tour d'Argent where we are right now. It was even once ranked the best restaurant in Tokyo. But it's also very convenient for me and my business. I always take the Hiroshige Presidential Suite. Your mother finds it very comfortable."

At this point I swallowed a big gulp of her Gevrey Chambertin. I couldn't believe my ears. "How long have you known my mother", I asked.

"Longer than I'd care to think my dear," he replied. "Well before she met your father, I visited Japan with my university, and met your mother at that time. You know, it was love at first sight for both of us. But her parents did not want her to marry a gaijin, especially since we were both young."

"Japan was still very, very traditional at the time. Most marriages were arranged either through families or the company. Your grandfather was working with your father, and introduced your father to your mother, and they were married soon after. I lost contact with your mother after that. Japanese wives devoted themselves to the home and family."

"But when your brother committed suicide, your mother was distraught and contacted me. She blamed it on your father who spent no time with the family. She found no comfort or solace with your father. I hope that you will forgive me for saying that he is like most Japanese men, he is a big baby, who wants his wife to be a substitute-mother."

"Your mother is a wonderful woman, intelligent, sophisticated, charming and very, very beautiful. Thankfully, I work in international business and can arrange my business travels to see your mother. Very few business leaders spend much time in Japan these days, we all go to China. But I can organize to myself to hop over to Tokyo and see your mother. We manage to get together at least once a month".

"Today, I love her more than I ever did. Like her, I married, and we had a family. I think of my children as your cousins. But we divorced. I am now totally devoted to your mother. I think of us like Prince Charles and Camilla, although your mother is much more beautiful than Camilla. We are two people who should have married when we were young, and will one day get married. We cannot avoid it."

"Even though you don't know me, I know you very well. You are a wonderful girl, just like your mother. You should be proud of your studies, a masters degree in sociology from the UGW is quite something. In my view, sociology is perhaps the most important subject of the 21st century. The challenge we all face is how to make our societies work better, and offer an opportunity to all of our citizens to lead a good life. This is true at the level of nations. But it is also true at the level of organizations like enterprises, government administrations and universities. Too many organizations are dysfunctional."

"I know that sociology is not highly valued in Japan, even though Japan's society is in desperate need of repair. It is dominated by men who don't give women the opportunity to succeed. And when women are given half a chance, the good women are dragged back down by the others who are jealous of anyone getting ahead of them. Japan is also dominated by the older generation. These seniors who get automatic pay rises and promotions, and who never retire are just clogging up the system. The consequence is that Japan now sees itself increasingly over taken by Korea and China."

"I know that you have a French boyfriend and that you will going back to Tokyo with him. But I would like to give you a chance in my company. You would not be working directly with me. I would put you in another team. You are just the type of person that my company needs. And it would certainly be much better for you to be working in my company than wasting your life in a coffee shop."

During the rest of the meal, Jean talked on and on about life in France and Europe, and how he saw the world developing. He firmly believes that the solution to the challenge of globalization is developing global citizens, people who can cross cultures and understand different points of view. "Mimi, you are just that, a global citizen, and I want to give you the chance that your own country cannot do. I know that you Japanese are cautious and don't rush into decisions. But think about, and give me a call when you get back to Japan."

I left Jean floating on a cloud. "This guy is amazing. He is so nice, kind, intelligent and cultivated. He loves my mother unconditionally. And it seems to be willing to do anything to help me."

When I arrived back at Eddie's apartment, he was preparing dinner. He started talking away in his own inimical way, and he seemed to have forgot that I was meeting with Jean. So I didn't say anything.

Mimi

Hi, it's Mimi. Tomorrow, Eddie and I leave for Paris. We have a big packing job to do. I also have to go back to the Hotel Dieu, and say farewell to the doctors and nurses. I convinced Eddie to come along with me.

In the metro going to the Hotel Dieu, I asked Eddie what was his blood type. He had no idea what I was talking about. In Japan and Korea, the first question a girl will ask a guy will be about his blood type. Some 90% of Japanese know their blood type. We are convinced that your blood type is a sure and sound indictor of your personality, temperament and compatibility with others. Japanese girls talk about it all the time, a bit like secretaries in the West talking about astrology and numerology.

Personally, I don't believe in astrology or numerology. But I am sure that blood type analysis is valid. It is your own real blood after all. I am type A, the most common blood type in Japan. Type As are typically obedient, careful, willing to compromise, honest and loyal, but we worry a lot, and we can be emotional, indecisive, introverted and nervous. It doesn't sound great, but that is Japan!

Then there is type B, the 'hunter' like Akira Kurosawa and Jack Nicholson. Type AB is the humanist like Marilyn Monroe and John F. Kennedy, while type O is the warrior like Queen Elizabeth II and John Lennon. I bet Eddie is a type O, if not a type B.

I said to Eddie, "go on, take a blood test at the Hotel Dieu to find out your blood type". He didn't want to. That is not a good sign for someone who should be a type O. So I nagged and nagged and nagged him. Eventually, he gave in.

When we arrived at the Hotel Dieu, all my old friends were there. They were very happy to see me, and to see that I had recovered from Paris Syndrome. We chatted, and promised to remain in touch. I realized that in fact we didn't have much in common now that I am well again.

I asked them if Eddie could do a blood test to discover his blood type. Of course, no problems.

Sacre bleu! Satori! Confit de canard!

Eddie is a type A just like me. But not only like me, also like George Bush Senior, Soseki Natsume, Ringo Starr, Britney Spears and Adolf Hitler!

This is not a good sign.

Hiddey

I was just coming back from the library at the UGW, and looked into a local Doutor coffee shop and there was my father.

I hesitated, but then entered. I had never really felt comfortable in my father's company, even though we are both academically inclined. In fact, I didn't recall ever having a long conversation with him.

Being an academic, not a salaryman, my father would not go out drinking with his colleagues at night. Sometimes, he would go out drinking with his students. But usually, he would go home in the evening.

It was pretty boring in the evening at our place. My mother would watch the television, while my father would read books. No-one spoke much. I usually go into my room and play computer games. Sometimes I would read, but mostly I would play computer games. I love computer games. They allow me to let go in a way that was not possible in real life.

But I am not really an "otaku" (a "nerd") like those guys down at Akihabara. True, I am a little uncomfortable in the company of girls. But I would never go to those maid cafes where the young servers dress up as maids. I am much more brave. I love erotic massage, and have discovered a Chinese massage service which was much cheaper than the regular Japanese ones.

I said to myself, "this is clearly one of the benefits of globalization, international competition is bringing down prices so that even young students like me can afford such pleasures."

My father was surprised to see me, but was strangely relaxed. I had never seen my father like that before. The students would say "hi" to him as they walked by. I thought that he seems a pretty cool guy.

We started chatting, not really like father and son, but more like teacher and student. We talked about my studies. We also talked about my experience at JINCS. I didn't express my views too strongly. I didn't feel comfortable enough to do that.

This inspired my father in a way that I had never seen before.

"You're perfectly correct, Hiddey, Japanese society is exactly like this. It is so hierarchical and class based. You may not have noticed, because it is so instinctive to us, but the first thing we Japanese do when we meet someone, is find out their age. There are many direct and indirect ways of finding out their age. But this is necessary, because it determines the way we speak, and the language that we use. We always use a more polite form of language for people who are older than us."

"But age is just one aspect of our feudal hierarchical system which poisons the way that people relate to each other. All cultures have social stratification and hierarchies – America's hierarchy is basically related to money. But as economies and societies develop, modernize and democratize, old traditional hierarchies tend to disappear, and there is greater equality between people. Japan is unique in the sense that our economy has developed, but our society has not really modernized."

"Back in the Edo period, before the black ships of Commodore Perry arrived, we had a strict hierarchy with four main classes or castes, I should really say. The samurai were at the top of the social hierarchy, followed by the peasants and the artisans, with the merchants at the bottom. Life was very safe and secure because you were not allowed to change your social class. But this strict hierarchy gradually broke down as the merchant class became more prosperous, as some samurai became financially dependent on them, and as the government became corrupt and incompetent. This was the real reason for the Meiji Restoration, not the arrival of the Americans. Wise Japanese wanted the Americans to put pressure on our creaking system of governance."

"Of course, today's social hierarchy is very different in many ways. But it is still a system of hierarchy that crushes certain classes and people – like women, youth, migrant groups like the Koreans and so on. Our social system is also morally bankrupt. Look at our country after two decades of crisis. We need a new Meiji Restoration. It will come, I believe it, but it will take time."

"In Edo times, there were other groups that did not fit into the main social hierarchy system, people like the "burakumin", for example. The burakumin are Japan's untouchables. Yes, like India, we have our untouchables. These poor people did the dirty work, they were leather workers, grave keepers, people who cleaned the toilets, or horse handlers. Japan considered them impure, even though many of them became very rich from this dirty work."

"The regrettable thing is that the descendants of these burakumin are still indentified and discriminated against today. No-one knows for sure, but there may be around 3 million burakumin in Japan today.

"And Hiddey, there is one thing that I have always wanted to tell you, but never had the courage. I am a descendant of a burakumin family. I suffered enormous discrimination when I was a kid in Osaka. That's why I went to study in the US, because I thought that I could escape such discrimination. During one of my school holidays, I visited Tokyo and met your mother, just by chance. It was love at first sight when we met in the library at the UGW in September 1985. Your mother had just lost her parents in the most terrible plane accident, the Japan Airlines Flight 123 from Tokyo to Osaka."

"We married almost instantly, and she came with me to the US. She loved the US, and that was where you were born, of course. One day I mentioned to your mother that I was a burakumin, and she fell into a deep state of shock. Families usually do a detailed check of the background of potential marriage partners. But since her parents had just been killed and she was an only child, no-one did a check up on me."

"At that point, I had basically finished my PhD. And following the shock of finding out my burakumin status, all your mother wanted to do was go home back to Japan. She accused me of lying and deceiving her. Although I didn't lie explicitly, it is true that I didn't tell her everything. But I feared that if I told her truth that she would never marry me, and I hoped that after we married that she would forgive me, and forget it."

"But no. We have since lived together, and brought you up. But we are no longer married in any meaningful sense. I was lucky to find a job here at the UGW through an old friend of mine who knew of my burakumin status. But I have never been able to get a promotion. This is why I am still just a lecturer to this very day."

"The Japanese people don't realize the full implications of sticking with social outcast groups. It is not just the burakumin, it is also all the Korean descendants of the people we forcibly moved here during Japan's colonization of Korea. We outcasts could contribute so much to this country. Most of us want to be full members of this society. Take the case of Hiromu Nonaka who was chief cabinet secretary in the government of the late 1990s. He should have become Prime Minister of Japan, but this was blocked by the old guard who were defending our stupid caste system."

"This also many negative implications for our society. It should not be surprising that most members of the Japanese mafia, the yakuza, are burakumin or Koreans. What do you expect? You treat people poorly, and they will turn against the society. Many of our neighbors are still pushing Japan to apologize sincerely for all of our war crimes. They are right. But the biggest apology that should be made is to our own people. First of all, the Japanese government should apologize to its own people for having led into a destructive and unwinnable war. It should also apologize to all minority groups like the burakumin and the Koreans. We should be given full rights, and it should launch a program of affirmative action to ensure equal treatment."

"I am sorry to burden you with all this now. But one day, sooner or later, you would have found out. It is something that you will have to live with. I can only recommend that you leave Japan. But rather than going to the US as I did, you should go to Europe, a country like France. Europe is so rich with culture. And although Europe has its own problems of racism, Europeans would never understand something as obscure as the burakumin."

My father placed his hand on my wrist. We looked at each other. Both our eyes welled up with tears. At long last, I felt that he was a real father.

Mimi and Eddie

Mimi and Eddie flew off to Tokyo with Japan Airlines.

"One flight with Air France was too much", Mimi said to herself, "I think that it was the terrible flight that caused my Paris Syndrome."

Eddie and Mimi were listening to the music on the flight entertainment system.

As they were relaxing, she was day dreaming.

"Japan Airlines is a bit like Air France quite frankly", she thought, "it is so inefficient that the Japanese government has to keep bailing it out. Staff are overpaid, and of course the senior management get big fat salaries. The planes are also old models. But at least you get Japanese service."

"After a few weeks in France, it was so nice to get back to Japanese service. The flight stewards bow all the time. They are forever asking us if we needed anything. And being in business class, we can have anything we wanted. All things considered, it's great to be leaving France"

"I can't wait to get back to Tokyo and see my friends again. I really missed Dutor. I wonder what the special Milano sando is this month, chicken or beef. And I can't wait to have a green tea latte, 'mache latte'."

They started with champagne. When the food menu came around, Mimi noticed once again confit de canard.

"No way, I 've had enough of confit de canard", she said to herself. So she ordered sushi followed by grilled salmon. With a glass of Japanese beer, it was perfect.

After the meal, they both dozed off. As they were both dreaming, the plane was suddenly jolted by some sharp turbulence. The stewards announced that everyone should buckle their seatbelts and stay in the seats.

Mimi shook Eddie, "quick, follow me to the toilet," she said.

Eddie thought that Mimi must be sick. They both rushed into the toilet, and then Mimi started kissing him. She was caressing his body all over, and then undid his trousers. She lifted her skirt, and then they started making love.

When they returned to the seats, Mimi said:

"You know, Eddie, I once read a book on Japanese eroticism which spoke of the excitement of making love when there is an earthquake. I always wondered if airplane turbulence is not the closest thing to the sensation of an earthquake."

After the episode with the duck at Giverny, Eddie was less surprised, and enjoyed this moment of intimate excitement, even though he was still half asleep.

When they arrived in Tokyo, Eddie went to the hotel that the UGW had booked him at Shibuya, just around the corner from the university campus. Mimi went home, and found her bedroom just as it was before she left. It was strange that everything should be just the same, but that she should feel so different now.

When her mother arrived home, she could instantly see that something had happened to Mimi. Mimi had already told her mother that she had met someone, but Mimi's mother was not expecting to see Mimi's new serenity and grace. Mimi talked vaguely of her lunch with Jean, but without mentioning any intimate details. Mimi's mother could feel the new complicity between them.

Eddie came around to Mimi's parents' apartment for dinner that evening, although Mimi's father was not there. Mimi's mother, Aiko, was pleased to meet him, and found him a nice French boy. She was very happy that her daughter should find love and affection in French man, just as she had.

When Mimi said that she would take Eddie to his hotel, Aiko made clear that she would not wait up for her. Mimi loved Eddie's hotel room. It was quite trendy in design, with lots of Japanese gadgets.

They lied down on the bed and began caressing each other. Then all of a sudden, the bed started moving, as if there was a jackhammer underneath it. Mimi quickly undressed and pounced on Eddie and began making love. The earthquake tremors subsided for a few minutes. And then suddenly there was a jolt, which seemed to shake the whole building. Mimi let go the loudest of screams as she climaxed. Poor Eddie was caught between fear and sexual excitement.

The earthquake then seemed to have passed. Mimi who now seemed to exude a new maturity and self-assurance started speaking to Eddie.

"You know Eddie, about 20 per cent of the world's earthquakes take place in Japan because it is sitting on the boundaries of at least three tectonic plates. And these earthquakes have left deep marks on the Japanese personality."

"In 1923 Great Kantō earthquake struck Tokyo and the surrounding region. Over 100,000 people were killed by this quake which struck the Kantō plain on Honshū on September 1, 1923 with a magnitude of 8.3 on the Richter scale. Tokyo, Yokohama and nearby prefectures were devastated. 60 per cent of Tokyo's population was left homeless. This earthquake lives on in the memory of many older Japanese people who remember it or who were constantly told of it by their parents."

"Some experts argue that another big earthquake was due 60 years after the Great Kanto quake, others argue for 80 years. Whatever the case, another great earthquake is long overdue. Tokyo is located near a fault line beneath the Izu peninsula. We never talk about earthquakes, but we are all scared."

"Many Tokyo residents who had been lulled into a false sense of security were awaken to their Damoclean Sword by the Great Hanshin earthquake, which struck Kobe on 17 January 1995. This was Japan's worst earthquake since the Great Kantō earthquake, and killed over 6,000 people and felled some 200,000 buildings. According to the Guinness Book of Records, it was the costliest natural disaster to befall any one country."

"Eddie, you may have heard of the contemporary Japanese novelist Haruki Murakami. After the Hanshin earthquake, he was inspired to write a collection of short stories, "After the Quake", revealing some of the psychological marks of the Kobe earthquake. Predictably, they are stories of urban alienation and social disintegration. But they also give an insight into what an emotional disturbance earthquakes must be for the Japanese people."

"The first story, 'UFO in Kushiro', is about Komura, a hi-fi equipment salesman in Tokyo's Akihabara "Electronics Town". After five straight days watching the effects of the quake on television, his wife disappears leaving a note which says 'you have nothing inside that you can give me'. "

"The Japanese government, and foreign embassies, are over abundant in advice for dealing with earthquakes. But after reading Murakami's stories, I don't think anything can prepare the mind and spirit for a big earthquake."

Eddie

I was so excited to visit the UGW, and see my new working environment. I telephoned the dean's office to make an appointment for a courtesy call.

When I arrived at UGW, I was received by the coordinator of international studies, a nice girl called Tanaka-san. She told me that I would be teaching two courses on cross cultural management. She was convinced that my knowledge of French language and interest in Japanese culture provided the perfect cocktail for cross cultural management. This course was part of UGW's international program. I would have about forty students from Asian countries like China, Hong Kong, Japan, Korea, Malaysia and Singapore, as well as a good number from North America, especially from California and Hawaii. There could be one or two Latin Americans of Japanese origin, mainly from Brazil and Peru.

I was of course flattered. Our French eyes always light up when the word culture is mentioned. The French have always believed that their global mission is to civilize the rest of the world, and to teach others how to speak their beautiful language.

But then I started to think a little. My training is in international finance and trade. I have no real experience in management. And although I love culture, especially Japanese anime and manga, I had only taken an introductory course in Asian culture and had been perplexed at the vast cultural diversity in Asia with all its different religions and systems of philosophy. I also noticed that there would be no European students in his class. They could have been an anchor for me.

I asked Tanaka-san if cross-cultural management was really the right course for me. She said that UGW always uses young short-term professors as stop-gaps, to fill in holes in their program. The previous young professor from France taught the history of women's rights, even though he did his PhD in physics.

"Don't worry, just go in and do your own thing", she said, "it will be right. Japanese students are passive and they attend very few classes anyway. And the foreigners are just here for fun. Bytheway, can you please send me your syllabus, with a detailed reading list, by next week. We have to provide this information to students to enable them to make their preferred choice of subjects".

I asked when I would be able to meet with the dean. Tanaka-san said that the dean was a very busy man, and does not accord meetings with visiting professors. "In Japanese universities, we have a very strict hierarchy. Don't worry, you will meet several other visiting professors very soon, as you will be sharing an office with three of them. They will be very good company for you."

I was a bit astonished by my welcome at UGW. "Who the hell are these people who bring me half way across the world, and then treat me like nothing," I said to himself. As I left the university, I noticed a coffee shop across the road. It was called Doutor. "I think that is the chain that Mimi works for". I entered the Doutor coffee shop. After puzzling my way through the list of drinks, I eventually ordered a "mache" green tea latte. "It tastes nice, sort of bitter-sweet, it must be a symbol of Japan!"

"What the hell," I said to myself. "I'm just here for fun. It's only one semester. And all I'm interested in is Japanese contemporary culture. It's high time I went to Akihabara, Tokyo's 'electric town'. It's also a good moment to test my skills on the Tokyo metro system.

If I get lost, I can always ask one of those little Japanese girls. They look just so cute."

Masa

I reserved a beautiful table at the la Tour d'Argent restaurant at the New Otani Hotel. I had heard that it was the best French restaurant in Tokyo.

Miyuki was so happy when we arrived. It was just so beautiful. She had read in a magazine at her newsstand about the famous duck. I ordered champagne to start. Miyuki drank it so quickly. Was it nerves or just thirst that made her drink so quickly?. In fact, she was not really accustomed to drinking. After two glasses she had rather pink cheeks but was still sort of in control of her senses.

The champagne and delightful atmosphere made us forget that this was a dinner of reconciliation. And Miyuki, who was usually quite reserved, became very talkative. She told me her tales of woe at her previous job, and how she felt obliged to leave after suffering sexual harassment. She also told me of the hardship of working in her little newsstand.

I wondered aloud why Miyuki had never got married. She emptied her sack of stories for me. When she was younger, she had many boyfriends, but those relationships led nowhere. She was a country girl, from Morioka in fact. She moved down to Tokyo after school to find an office job ("OL" or "office lady"). Being an out-of-towner, she never had the usual family connections in Tokyo, which often lead to arranging of marriages between young people. Then she had a few American boyfriends, guys who lived on the military bases near Yokohama.

The American boyfriends were fun, even though they were loud and boisterous. They had lots of money to take her out. But most of them were on short stays of duty, usually two years. Then they would head to another assignment. There was one, however, "Hank", who Miyuki really loved. He actually stayed for five years. She took him back to Morioka to meet her family. But being country folks, her family would not accept a foreigner, a "gaijin", as a husband of their daughter. Hank actually proposed to Miyuki, and offered to take her back to Texas to live with him. Her parents put her under immense pressure to stay.

Miyuki never got over this. She said that she still thinks of Hank to this very day. She heard word that Hank married another Japanese girl. He must have a thing about Japanese girls, some men do. Apparently they are very happily married, and have two children.

By this point, Miyuki was in tears. The alcohol and the emotions had got to her. We finished the meal quietly. I was touching her feet with mine. Japanese men never do this. But I had never known such intimacy before, and felt almost childlike. I started crying too. I don't know why. When we finished the meal with champagne, we were both decidedly drunk.

As we left the restaurant, Miyuki had fallen into my arms. I was virtually carrying her out.

Aiko

Jean and I were just about to enter the la Tour d'Argent restaurant, and what do we see through the front door? There was my husband Masa in the arms of a drunken women.

I pulled Jean away from the restaurant, and dragged him back up to his room. I said to myself, "this is it, it's over, I now have solid grounds for divorce".

Aiko

I guess that I am like most Japanese housewives. I manage the household budget and provide my husband with his monthly pocket money after I have received his monthly salary. I would also be regarded as a very astute investor. I read Japan's business newspaper the Nikkei daily, and follow stock markets and exchange rates closely.

Quite frankly, I am convinced that household financial management is the natural role of Japanese women. Japanese men are reckless and irresponsible with money. But more than that, I believe that, when it comes to investing in financial markets, women have a clear edge on men. As we see with all these financial crises, financial markets are fundamentally irrational. To understand markets, you don't need complicated economic analysis, you really need good intuition and feeling. And this is the Japanese woman's strong suit.

When I am studying markets in the newspaper and on the Internet, I can feel certain temperatures. It's almost spiritual. And when I am a bit confused, I consult a fortune teller. The streets and shopping malls of Tokyo are lined with fortune tellers. I was lucky enough to find a good one. This fortune teller does not understand financial markets at all. But she employs the vibration method. She asks me to talk about all the different investment options, and waits to feel the vibration in her stomach. This is a perfect predictor. For example, the day before the Lehman shock in September 2008 which provoked the global financial crisis, the fortune teller had a massive case of indigestion, a certain sign that something cataclysmic was going to happen. And sure enough, it did.

I have made a real killing on the financial markets. In fact, I am a much better investor than Jean, my friend from Paris. A few times, I have even had to lend him money to cover his bad investments.

I have always put some money aside in secret bank accounts in Switzerland. In Japanese, we call such secret savings "hesokuri". I also have an apartment in Paris in which Jean has been living since his divorce. More and more Japanese women are keeping private investments on the side, now that divorce is on the rise. In fact, it is estimated that more than one-third of Japanese marriages could today end in divorce. And contrary to what you might think, it is Japanese women who are the divorce activists.

Japanese women are now more educated than they were, and have higher aspirations for the life. They have also seen how the situation of women in America and Europe has changed. So many just say to themselves, why should I suffer like my mother did. I would prefer a good marriage and family. But being single is better than being married to man who is out drinking and womanizing all week, and has no time for the family.

Now with concrete proof of Masa's relationship with Miyuki, I concluded that this is the perfect moment for divorce. I could keep my money in Switzerland. No-one knows of this, not even Jean. And then I could get half of the other family assets. I went to see my lawyer, and told him to launch divorce proceedings. With that, I headed off to Zurich and Paris.

Eddie

I set off for Akihabara. I first took the metro and then changed for the JR line, Japan Railways. "They seem to have two rail systems like we do in Paris. I guess the JR is a bit like our RER". But as soon as I arrived on the JR platform, I felt like I was in another Japan. Everything seemed older and a bit shabby. Even the people looked somewhat downtrodden. When the train arrived, I thought it must have been built in the 1950s. I was having trouble getting a good feel for Tokyo.

When I arrived at Akihabara station, there was no mistaking where I was. Tokyo's electric land was fully alight with tall buildings covered in neon signs advertising electric products. It really had an atmosphere. As I looked more closely at the buildings, I thought that they all looked like cheap, modern high rise buildings.

"Tokyo really is not a beautiful city, like Paris", I said to myself. "In Paris, we have kept a lot of our old buildings, and there is a certain architectural harmony. Walking around is such a delight for the eyes, as you discover jewels of buildings here and there."

I realized that Tokyo has very few remaining old buildings, and there is no apparent attempt to create an architectural harmony. "Akihabara does have a great atmosphere nonetheless." But what also struck me was that as soon as you walk off the main street, it almost seemed like a developing country. It actually reminded me of Marrakesh where I had been on family holidays.

As I walked down the street, I noticed many of the famous Japanese "otaku", these nerds whose life passion is manga, anime and computer games. They were just as I imagined, sloppily dressed, shy-looking and expressionless. In short, they looked just like nerds.

I had been dying to see a maid café. And sure enough, before too long, I was approached in the street by one of these young girls dressed up as a maid, trying to coax innocent young boys into their café. I followed her up to the café which was full of these young girls, otaku and young salary-men. There was a very clear sign indicating that you cannot touch the maids or ask them for their personal details. The maids were running around talking and giggling in stupid, high squeaky voices. As they served each customer, they would stay a while and talk. You could have your photo taken with a maid for 2,000 yen. She then signed the photo in nail polish saying that she is "turned on" and that she loves you. This was the maid-game, or so it seemed.

Walking down the street, I noticed groups of what seemed to be Chinese tourists. I know the sound of the Chinese language. And even though they look a little like the Japanese, you can clearly distinguish them. They are talkative, noisy and full of life, not uptight, reserved and expressionless. They really seemed to be having a good time.

I went into some of the shops and had a look around. I went to the computer games counter to see what they had. It was strange, they didn't seem to have all the latest American computer games. I had heard that the Americans had picked many of Japan's ideas and developed new games. It's strange that the US should now be copying and perfecting Japanese innovations. In the 1960s and 1970s, Japan used to be the copycat nation.

I also noticed a big group of Chinese tourists lining up at one counter. The shop assistant was speaking with them in Chinese. The Chinese tourists left the shop with bags and bags of purchases. "China really seems to be putting life into the Japanese economy," I said to myself.

I walked further down the main street, Chūō-dōri, and noticed a massage parlor. A few girls were standing in the street, beckoning customers into the parlor. They even spoke to me in English. I thought to himself, "why not", and followed one of the girls. When I arrived in the parlor, I realized that all the girls were Chinese.

The girl I followed then asked what type of massage I would like: with or without oil; one, two or three hours; and would I like an "option".

"What do you mean by option?", I asked. She pinched me on the buttocks and said, "come on, you know what I mean".

The Chinese masseur was very friendly and talkative, quite different from the maids at the café who were dressed up like dolls and were almost robotic in their movements. Her name was Sandy, she came from north-east China. I didn't ask any more questions of her. I just laid back and enjoyed her fingers running all over me, as she found every nook and cranny of stresses and tensions in my body. I couldn't understand, but this sensual massage was somehow much more erotic than making love with Mimi.

After the massage, I decided to walk up to Ginza, which I had heard so much about. It wasn't very far away. The Ginza looks great, lots of luxury class shops and beautiful people. In fact, it seems more classy than our Champs Elysees.

Again, I saw more buses of Chinese tourists. Some of the luxury shops were full of them. They seemed to be buying lots of things.

I bought a newspaper, the Nikkei Weekly, the main English language business and economics newspaper. I noticed another Doutor coffee shop. I sat down, had a mache latte and started reading the newspaper.

The headline story was all about the Chinese government's recent substantial purchases of Japanese Government Bonds. Following the global financial crisis, and China's concerns about having too much money tied up in US Treasury Bonds, China is now looking for other investment opportunities. With Europe also mired in a sovereign debt crisis, there is no better investment opportunity than Japanese Government Bonds.

There was another article on China's new business tycoons buying real estate and companies in Japan. "This makes sense," I said to myself, "such investments are a good way for China's nouveau riche to hedge their bets, in case the Chinese Communist Party collapses."

I was struck by this. I already knew that China was Japan's biggest trading partner. Could this be the shape of things to come? Could China virtually take over Japan one day?

Mimi

I was so happy to return to Doutor and see all of my friends again. I instantly got back into the swing of serving coffees, teas, sandwiches and cakes. It's kinda fun.

But after a few days, I became a little bored. My colleagues seemed rather naïve and almost virginal. So childlike, really.

I knew that I could not last in Doutor for too long. I needed a project, a dream. Something to lift my spirit. I hadn't realized until then the effect of my trip to Paris.

"What will all these Doutor staff members be doing in 30 years time?", I said to myself, "still working for Doutor? They probably will be because none of them have any plans or ambitions. And none of them now have any other opportunities open to them."

I did however feel more attracted to Sandy. She has great personal depth. She seems to know what she is doing. She seems to have some experience of life.

"I will wait until Eddie's teaching assignment is finished at the UGW", I thought. "Perhaps I could then return to Paris with him. I could even take up that job offer that Jean made to me."

Then I thought again, "the longer Eddie stays in Japan, the more he is becoming like those boring Japanese otakus. I will have to wait and see. But I will have to do something."

Masa

It is Saturday morning. I woke up with a terrible hangover following a big drinking session last night. Yesterday, my boss told me that the company's senior management had agreed to my request to an oversea posting. I would be sent to New Delhi India, where I was expected to develop new markets and manage the office. Japan and India had recently signed a free trade agreement which opened new possibilities for doing business. It would be a good opportunity to diversify out of the China market on which my company had become overly reliant. I had to leave within two weeks to get this important project launched.

This is a disaster. All my dreams of spending evenings in the girly bars of Vietnam or Thailand were shattered. I can't stand Indian women at all. They are usually overweight, and they smell of curry. What's more, they talk all the time.

And when it comes to doing business, Indians are the most difficult of all. You can't avoid long, tortuous negotiations. And the day after you agree on something, the Indians will come back and try to reopen the negotiations.

Korean companies like Samsung and LG have stolen a march on Japanese companies in India, and my management would like me to get back some market share. But these Korean companies had brought many Indian staff members into the local branch to help with designing products for local markets, and to lead the marketing efforts. I certainly do not like the idea of having foreigners as colleagues with virtually the same level of responsibility. Japanese companies are used to having foreigners work in their factories, but certainly not as managers.

And like most Japanese, I do not speak very good English. I do not relish the challenge of trying to understand the Indian's funny accents and convoluted logic.

As I sat down to breakfast, I could feel a certain emptiness in the apartment. I went over to the kettle to make some green tea, and noticed an envelope with my name on it. I wondered what it could have been, and how long it could have been there. As I recalled, I hadn't taken breakfast at home at all this week. I had rushed out in the morning and had breakfast at the local Doutor coffee shop.

I opened the envelope with a slight sense of trepidation. It had a lawyer's name and address on it.

I started reading "Our client Madame Aiko Watanabe has asked us to represent her in your forthcoming divorce case …".

I read the note again and again. "What will my friends and colleagues say and think? How will Mimi react?" These were the words that I kept repeating to myself.

My wife and I had not been close for a very long time, if we ever were. We didn't socialize any more. We virtually never saw each other. We had separate bedrooms. And when we bumped into each other in the kitchen, we would barely acknowledge each other.

A divorce would give me greater freedom to spend time with Miyuki. "But what will my friends and colleagues say and think? How will Mimi react?" I kept repeating these words to myself.

I sat down, and started thinking. "How will the assets be divided? Will I have a place to live? Yes, India, but that is the last place where I would like to live."

I was becoming dizzy. I kept standing up and sitting down. I began sweating profusely. I was twitching. My right shoulder kept going up and down.

Who could I speak to? I didn't really have any friends, just colleagues to drink with. I had never shared any personal thoughts or feelings with them, nor with anyone. Could I speak with Mimi? She wouldn't understand.

I decided to call Miyuki. She wasn't answering. Eventually, she called me back. I wasn't quite sure how long after. I had lost track of time.

We agreed to have dinner that evening. I suggested a Japanese sushi restaurant. I needed to drink some saki. That goes well with sushi.

Sandy

I am just sitting, taking a break from massaging, and reading a Chinese newspaper. It's hard work physically as you have be on your feet in the street, scouting for customers. And then of course, massaging itself is hard work. Since most of the Japanese customers are so stressed out, they want hard massages to relieve their tension.

I just noticed an article on Chinese girls who married Japanese farmers. It dealt with in particular the marriage business in the farm areas around Nigata on the western seaboard of Honshu. The local municipal government used to be very active in organizing such marriages with Chinese, Filipino and Thai girls. But since the Chinese are so enterprising, a Chinese agency started to get involved in this business. They would bring over girls from China, and the Japanese farmers who had difficulty finding wives could obtain a young Chinese wife.

It seemed like a good business for everyone. The girls would have a much better life than living in poverty at home. The Japanese farmer would have companionship and someone to look after him. If the farmer dies before the wife, she can inherit all his wealth and send it home to her family. It was often a very good deal because the farmers were usually much older than the girls. There are even some rumors of Chinese girls murdering their husband to get the money! The agency gets a cut on both sides – both the girls and the famers would pay a commission.

The main downside was the language barrier. But Japanese men don't talk much anyway. And with the growing number of foreign brides, they would all get together once a day at the local Doutor café after they had done their shopping.

I thought to myself, "this would be perfect. I could live up there in Nigata and finish my thesis and create my migrant support organization. If my future husband is a disaster, I could just escape. With a bit of luck he might just drop dead."

Through my Chinese network, I found the contact details of the Chinese agent, and called them. They welcomed my interest, and asked me to come up to Nigata next week.

I was picked up at the station, and driven to an apartment block and escorted to an apartment. Going up the staircase, I could hear lots of Chinese being spoken, and could detect the stale smell of dumpling broth. "This seems to be a Chinese-owned apartment block", I surmised.

Inside the apartment, I was received by a man of about 50 years age, overweight with a big, round belly. He was not unpleasant, but very sharp and direct. He explained how the marriage works. I would have to pay $5000 to the agency for the marriage, and have to guarantee to stay with the husband for at least two years. As part of the deal, the future husband also pays $5000. At the moment, they only have one candidate, a certain Makoto who is 65 years old, and has a good chance of dying within the next ten years.

I agreed to meet Makoto. He seemed to be a kind, pleasant old man. He looked very tired and somewhat overweight. He had lived with his parents on the farm until their death one year ago, but he had never married. With his parents passing, he finds himself all alone, and in need of household help. He wasn't expecting a romantic marriage, just friendship, companionship and household help.

I agreed to think about it, but quickly decided that it was a good deal. I would be provided for by Makoto, and could continue to send my scholarship money to my parents. And thank goodness, I could leave my position at Doutor and also give up the massage work.

Makoto and I were married at the local prefectural office, and I moved in with him the following week. I moved up all of my university books and research materials, and arranged for high speed Internet access. Makoto didn't have a computer.

Eddie

A few days after meeting the course coordinator at the UGW, I met my fellow young visiting professors. Pierre was also from France, Sonya from Italy and Manfred from Germany. They were a warm friendly bunch.

After exchanging greetings, I tried to understand better how UGW operates. I broached the subject indirectly by mentioning that I would be teaching cross cultural management, and yet I was basically an international economist. The others burst into laughter. They had all had similar experiences. Pierre is a philosophy major teaching industrial relations, Sonya is an economist but she is teaching marketing, and Manfred is a history major who is teaching social stratification.

They had all had the same experience. What counts most of all is that you can speak English. UGW is expanding rapidly into international education, and is desperately in need of professors. Also since their budget is tight, they have been bringing in young Europeans on trainee visas, and paying them the bare minimum. They figure that young professors will put up with anything for a while.

The other visiting professors all recommended that I get a feel for the class before deciding on how to teach the students. The typical Japanese professor just stands there reading lectures. Another approach is to have a seminar style class with class presentations and guest lecturers. I said to myself that this might be the best model for a group of international students. I could get a cross cultural dialogue going between the students.

For my first class, I did just this, getting them all to express themselves. My class was made up of one-quarter Japanese, one-quarter Americans, one-quarter Chinese and one-quarter for the rest. Quite predictably, the American kids were very good expressing themselves, and very interesting in discovering the mysteries of Japanese management. After two decades of crisis, was there anything left in the Japanese model -- all the more so given that Korean companies like Samsung had now overtaken most big Japanese companies.

The Chinese kids were also quite vocal. Although their mastery of English was not so good, they were not frightened of expressing themselves. They fluctuated between being very defensive of China and its government, and insisting that China still has a long way to go before it becomes a developed country. Most of the other foreign students were also pretty active. By contrast, the Japanese kids were more reluctant to speak.

I kept this pattern of having a highly interactive teaching style. The foreign students relished this, but like most foreigners in Japan became increasingly vocal in their criticism of Japan.

After the second class, I went to a local bar for a drink, and found most of the foreign students there, and so I joined them. So every week thereafter, I would go drinking with the students. They were rousing sessions of heated discussions, and rowdy behavior. Most of them would be rather drunk by the end.

I would usually then take the metro back to my apartment, and a few students would share part of the journey with me. One evening, there was just one Chinese student accompanying me, "Jane" from Shanghai. One thing led to another and we spent the evening together.

We agreed to keep our relationship secret, but without knowing it, we had been seen together by the course coordinator.

Following this, I received a call from the course coordinator to see her. I had been fired. No intimate relations with the students were permitted.

What would I say to Mimi with whom I am still romantically involved? Would I stay in Japan? And above all what would I do with Jane for whom I now felt an intense passion?

As I was packing my bags, I discussed all this with my fellow visiting professors. They agreed that this could be a blessing in disguise. Teaching in Japan is not such a great thing. Japanese higher education is in crisis.

I should stay in Japan and have fun for the remainder of my visa. If I needed some money, they recommended that I get a job teaching English. There were lots of private schools offering short term positions.

Sandy

I was looking forward to moving in with Makoto. I thought that it would be nice and peaceful to live in the country. I was also looking forward to getting my teeth into my thesis.

The first few days of marriage were a bit awkward. We were not used to each other's company. He mainly liked soup and soba noodles, so I cooked that for him every night. I kept the house very clean. In fact, it looked as if hadn't been cleaned for a long, long time. Makoto would have a little saki each evening, but that's all.

I started my research in earnest for my thesis. The topic was the state of Chinese immigration into Japan. This information would help me understand the needs of the Chinese community and how my migrant support organization could help.

I had a sense that there was a growing number of Chinese people in Japan. You hear Chinese being spoken everywhere. Over the ensuing couple of months, I would document in detail the state of Chinese migration in Japan. Since the beginning of time there have been Chinese people in Japan. And over the centuries and decades, there have been several waves. But historically, Chinese migration into Japan has never been very important. On the contrary, the main migrant group has been the Koreans, many of whom were forcibly transported to Japan during its occupation of Korea in the first half of the twentieth century.

But when Deng Xiaoping opened China's borders to international trade and investment in 1978, it also opened the way for migration. In fact, Chinese migrants are now virtually flooding the world. Sometimes they are legal, sometimes illegal, sometimes they are tourists who don't return, and sometimes they are students like me who don't return. Despite its rapid growth, China still has so many poor people who are desperate to find a better life. China also has lots of migration entrepreneurs who facilitate human smuggling, human trafficking and other forms of illegal migration.

Over the past couple of decades, Japan's migrant population has more than doubled to over two million people. Most of them are illegal, and they do the jobs that Japanese people do not want to do. These Chinese migrants do not cause any problems. Like most Chinese, they are very pragmatic and mainly want to make money.

My research made me think about the agency that organized my marriage to Makoto. The agency kept in touch with me, and followed my relationship with Makoto. It also asked me for contacts with other Chinese girls who might want to marry a Japanese farmer. I did recommend a few who in fact went through with these organized marriages. As I delved deeper and deeper into my research, I found a reference to the agency in one website. It seemed to allege that the agency was involved in human trafficking with the Chinese mafia. I felt a little nervous that I might be falling into their web of business.

I had also done quite a bit of research on how to set up a migrant support organization in Japan. Although the procedure seemed quite complex, I concluded that all that was needed was immense patience. But the more I thought about the migrant support organization idea, the more I felt fearful of the agency.

As time rolled on, life with Makoto was not quite as easy going as at the beginning. He drank a lot, more and more. And he was putting on more weight. It got to the point where every night he would get drunk. And when he was really screaming drunk, he would run around and around our living room yelling "Showa, Showa". I later learnt that this was the name of the previous Japanese emperor, who had reigned during the time of World War 2.

When Makoto did this, I would go into my bedroom and lock it. Makoto would never direct aggression at me, but he still made me feel nervous. Eventually he would pass out through the combination of drunkenness and exhaustion. The next morning, he would always seem in good form, and also have no apparent memory of the drunken behavior. In fact, the morning after he would usually be as gentle as a kitten. I learnt a long time ago to never confront Japanese people over anything that might seem embarrassing.

Eddie

I packed up my personal effects, and prepared to leave the UGW.

As I was departing the office, I bumped into Jim, an older Australian guy who had been teaching at UGW for many years. I had heard about Jim. He was obviously a wizened old survivor who knew how to work the Japanese system. As soon as we started talking, I could sense Jim's capacity to play the Japanese hypocrisy game. Bowing down to authority. Never expressing your point of view. Never contradicting anyone. And letting the Japanese feel that they are in control.

Jim told me not to worry about being fired. "They are just making an example of you. They need you young professors to conduct their international courses. But they fear that you might be too independent in your thinking. They needed to find an excuse to fire someone to instill some discipline. The Japanese system works by fear. Any nail that sticks out must be hit back into place."

Jim obviously harbored many great frustrations from his time at the UGW. He went on to explain the great crisis of Japanese higher education. Japanese students are pushed to the limit at high school, and perform very well. The main problem is that the education system is based on rote learning, rather than developing critical thinking and analysis, or the capacity for oral and written expression. Most exams are based multiple choice questions rather than papers where they must demonstrate reasoning capacities. For example, Japanese high school history textbooks are the shortest in the developed world, but have by far the most dates!

There is a fierce competition to get into the best universities and courses. The law school at Tokyo University is the most prestigious. But the level of the university courses is not very high. In fact, university is basically a period of respite between the tough pressures of high school and the immense pressures of work life. When the best students start working in a big company or a government ministry, they go through intense training. The main purpose of this is to create "company men" or "organization men" who will be loyal and devoted throughout their whole career. The companies and government ministries are in fact quite happy that their recruits have not learned too much independent thinking at university. That means that they can mould their recruits very easily.

This system worked quite well in previous decades. But times have changed. The world of today needs people who are capable of deep specialization, real experts, not company men. But very few Japanese students ever do masters degrees or PhDs. This means that Japan is now falling way behind the Chinese, Koreans and Americans whose best students go on and do postgraduate studies and postdoctoral research.

In the old days, Japan's system of innovation worked well. They would take or copy knowledge from overseas, and perfect it and adapt it secretively inside their corporations. But the whole world of innovation has changed. Open innovation involving cooperation between different enterprises, universities and research institutes is leading the way. Inward looking company men are just incapable of working in such a way. What's more, international partnerships are the latest trend as multinational enterprises work across borders. But the Japanese are still very weak in the English language, which is more and more the language of international business and research. And less and less Japanese students go overseas to study, unlike the Chinese and Korean kids.

If you want to get a good sense of the innovative capacities of Japan, just look at the Japanese cuisine. Each cooking chef is specialized in one narrow area of cuisine, like sushi, tempura or shabu shabu. He might own a restaurant that serves only that. And because he is only preparing the one dish all the time, he never innovates, it is always the same thing. Sure, he might change one or two ingredients a little bit. Sure, it is always perfect, but it is always the same – all the more so given that each master chef learns from his master as an apprentice. Real progress is impossible in such a situation. To innovate, you need to be more opened minded. That's why the very few innovative Japanese chefs open restaurants in New York where you have more freedom to test new ideas.

Eddie

Jim had the following advice for me.

"Eddie, you should go off and enjoy yourself for the rest of your stay in Japan", said Jim. "Japan is a fascinating country. It is a strange mixture of the modern and the ancient. The country has this veneer of the hyper-modern. I am sure that you have been down to Akihabara to see electric city and Harajuku to see those cute young girls all dressed up."

"But the mindset of the people is archaic. When you read European medieval history, you really wonder how those people could have been like they were. In Japan, the mindset is still very medieval with all the hierarchy, ceremony and protocol. There is no other country in Asia like that. All of that stuff was lost in China through the civil war, communism and the Cultural Revolution. The Chinese are today very modern in their thinking."

"But while the Japanese may have kept all these social attitudes of the past, they have totally lost their spirit. When they opened up their country in the 19th century, they dedicated themselves to catching up the West, and really becoming a member of the West. By 1989, they had basically made it. But they have now spent much of the past two decades in economic crisis, and have now become the lost tribe of an otherwise dynamic Asia. Quite simply, they don't know where they are going, and the political leadership has no ideas."

"To see the spirit of ancient Japan, I would recommend that you go and spend some time in a temple Kamakura. I have an old Japanese friend who is a monk in a Buddhist temple, and he can receive you. He taught meditation for many years in America. His temple is just amazing. You should spent a month there, and he could recommend other temples to visit in Japan."

"Zen Buddhism is the real authentic spirit of ancient Japan. But today Japan does not believe in anything. And as China and Korea make more and more progress, Japan is becoming increasingly inward-looking and paranoid."

"Both Chinese and Korean have a great sense of self belief. The Koreans know they have achieved an economic miracle. They are very keen to avoid the mistakes of Japan. And unlike Japan, they are not big enough to succumb to the temptation of turning inward. They know that they have to compete internationally to succeed. And being squeezed between China and Japan is a great motivator. Sure, they are similar to Japan in terms of having a declining birth rate and population. But they recognize that they must be more open to migration."

"These Chinese have an immense sense of self belief. They have just overtaken Japan to become the world's second biggest economy. They are very conscious of how they suffered under Japanese and Western domination in the late 19th and first half of the 20th century. And they want to return to the world's centre stage. At the same time, they are fully aware that they are still a developing country with a long way to go."

"I don't know how Japan can survive in the future unless the nation finds a new sense of identity. The young kids seem lost. You must have noticed the difference between them and the foreign students in your class. The only scenario that I can imagine is paranoid nationalism being provoked by a sense of confusion due to the rise of China and Korea. And while the Americans will always be there to protect Japan, that only stops them from growing up."

"It's curious. Japanese men are the most immature that I have ever met because their wives behave like mothers. And Japan as a nation remains politically immature in large part because America is there as its big brother or father".

"Please forgive my digression into international relations. But I strongly recommend that you get out and spend some time in those Buddhist temples, and see and feel the spirit of ancient Japan."

I was greatly inspired by Jim's suggestion to spend some in a Buddhist temple at Kamakura. So I did some research on Kamakura and made a visit including to the monastery that Jim recommended. I thought that this was the ideal opportunity for forgetting my bad experience at the UGW.

It was also a good opportunity for taking some distance from Mimi who somehow seemed less attractive and less exotic now that we are both in Japan. I just told Mimi that things were not working out at the UGW and that I was going to explore some of the religious culture of Japan.

I visited Kamakura, and was greatly impressed by the Great Buddha, the Hasedera Temple and the Hachimangu Shrine. I was most impressed by the Kenchoji Zen temple, the most important and oldest of Kamakura's five great Zen temples which dates back to the thirteenth during the Kencho Era. In fact, its first head priest came from China. The influence of the Chinese on Japan is just amazing!

But what impressed me most from my research was the another Zen temple, much closer to Tokyo, the Sotoshu Daihonzan Sojiji Temple. I went to this temple and practiced "Zazen" which involves a combination of seated and walking meditation. Although I initially found the seated position very difficult, I got used to it, and progressively felt an inner calm take over my spirit. Although the temple was on the outskirts of an ugly small town, it was the most beautiful and serene place I had ever been too.

I found myself going there every day, and eventually the head monk suggested that I stay. Mimi was very surprised that her 'manga maniac' boyfriend should somehow to get involved in Buddhism. She really did not know much about it. Like most Japanese, she practiced both Shinto and Buddhist rituals as tradition dictates. But she really did not know much about either, and was not even really interested.

Hiddey

I have now basically finished my research for my thesis. I came to the firm conclusion that Japan's post-war economic model has run out of steam. It was a form of economic militarism which only knew how to march in one direction, but did not have the capacity to adapt to new global conditions and the challenges of new phases of economic development.

Building up industry based on close relationships between government, business and financial institutions was a system that worked. But as the yen rose in value, Japanese industry was increasingly hollowed out and shifted offshore. The government should have switched to liberalizing and developing a dynamic, innovation and service-based economy. Instead, the government pumped up the economy into a bubble which burst, and left much of the corporate and financial sectors bankrupt.

While these close and cosy relationships between government, business and financial institutions may have succeeded in getting the Japanese economy launched after the Second World War, these very relationships were holding the country back now. They are blocking the necessary changes in Japan's economic model. Not only are they dragging Japan down, the government tried to tackle the symptoms rather than the causes of Japan's economic problems by spending up big, leaving the country with an enormous public debt, the biggest debt in the modern world.

So why then did Japan make all these policy mistakes? What happened to the brilliant Japanese policy makers who engineered Japan's rise from the ashes of war?

These are difficult questions to answer. But fundamentally I have great doubts about the capacities of Japan's policy makers. They are typically law graduates from Tokyo University. This means that their natural instinct is to regulate everything.

They are rarely economics graduates who would be more concerned with having the right incentives for economic dynamism. They rarely undertake postgraduate studies, something considered an absolute necessity in the US. What's more, they usually have job rotations every two years, which means that they can avoid tackling major problems in the hope that nothing explodes before they move on. Usually they will leave difficult problems to their successors.

The Japanese system is dominated by a management system based more on seniority than meritocracy. The Japanese are inherently very conservative and very likely to avoid radical action even when it's necessary. And lastly, Japan's elite bureaucrats are deeply arrogant and imagine that they can control many economic outcomes. They forget that the economy is an organism which can sometimes have its own mind.

It is an immense tragedy that the Japanese economy is in its present awful mess. The great Japanese people deserve more than this!

I really wonder why the Japanese people has not risen up against their government, like the Egyptians are doing now. In other countries like France or China, there might have been a revolution.

I organized a meeting with my thesis supervisor before finalizing his draft. Before entering the supervisor's office, the secretary said:

"Your supervisor usually accepts a payment of one million yen from successful doctorate students and half a million from successful masters students. I hope that the next time you pass by you will have the necessary cash to ensure successful completion of your masters degree."

I was so wild with anger when I heard this that I could not speak. It did not put me in the right mood for meeting with my supervisor.

When I entered the supervisor's office, he had a very stern look on his face. "Tell me where you are up to in your research".

As I then proceeded to summarize my main conclusions to my supervisor I could see his face become red and then scarlet:

"This rubbishy research is totally unacceptable", he yelled, "you don't understand anything. You have been reading too many stupid books by American professors who have no idea of what's really happening in Japan. We are going through a 21st century renaissance, and will surpass China and America in a matter of years."

Following that, I stormed out of my supervisor's office, and never returned. The corruption and stupidity of Japanese academics is intolerable.

I later learned that my supervisor was granted a major position at the Ministry of Finance, "Little wonder he would not support my research!"

I thought back to my discussions with my father. Perhaps my father was right. It may be best for me to leave Japan. I also wondered if my supervisor had discovered my burakamin status.

Masa

I am standing on the platform at the Shibuya JR, Japan Railways, Station. Next week, I will leave for India. The very thought of India depresses me. What has my life come to? From my brilliant studies in law at Tokyo University, now I will be office manager for my company in New Delhi.

I am waiting for the train. The weather is hot and humid. I am sweating profusely. So many thoughts are running through my mind. My son's suicide. Mimi and her unstable life. Her relationship with Eddie has no future. And then my wife Aiko. How could she leave me? She has humiliated me in the eyes of all of my colleagues. I am sure that all of my colleagues are gossiping about my divorce. I am also sure that's why I am being sent to New Delhi. Even my bosses don't respect me any more.

The only positive thing in my life is my love for Miyuki. There is something motherly about her. She is kind, she listens to me. She is not really sexy. But that is almost better. She reminds me of my childhood with my mother and sister. I am not sure what love is, but I think that what I feel for Miyuki must be love. Now I have to leave her and go to New Delhi. I don't know how I will survive.

The sun is beating down at Shibuya station. I begin to feel dizzy with all these thoughts running through my mind. The train arrives. I try to move my legs to get on the train. But I feel stuck to the ground. All of my body is tense and tight. My shoulders are twitching uncontrollably. As I was stuck to the ground, I start to feel more confused. What is happening to me? Am I going to collapse? I feel faint.

The train left. I will take the next train. I am waiting for the next train. It seems to take ages to come. When will it arrive? I can't stand this tension and confusion at the railway station. I then hear the train in the distance.

I start to move my body in preparation for getting on the train. I manage to unlock my legs and motion toward the edge of the platform. The sound of the train grows louder and louder. I can see the train coming. It is now about to pull into the station. My body lurches forward and then jerks backwards. It then wobbles and staggers forward closer and closer to the edge of the platform. The heat, the confusion, all the crowds and now the noise of the arriving train are getting to me. I feel like I am losing consciousness of where I am for a moment.

Shibuya station

"Thud, crash, bang".

Legs and arms and pieces of Masa's body started flying in the air, as soon as his body hit the still fast moving train. The passengers waiting on the platform were splattered and showered with Masa's blood and small pieces of unidentifiable flesh.

There was chaos on the platform as the crowd whispered "suicide, suicide".

Miyuki

It was six o'clock in the morning. I was unbundling newspapers and magazines on the newsstand. I wondered if Masa would call me today. I wanted to see him as much as possible before his departure to India.

A copy of the Yomiuri Shimbun fell open. I never read newspapers, but this time my eyes ran down the open page. I saw an article about a Japanese businessman who was due to leave for India, and who had just committed suicide by diving onto the train line at Shibuya station. As I slowly absorbed this information, my body and legs began collapsing in the newsstand.

It must have been two days later that I slowly woke up in a hospital surrounded by my family who had come down from Morioka. I was confused. Where was I? What was happening? Where is Masa? Has he left for India? I was still under heavy sedation, and was very groggy.

I gradually started to pull together all the pieces of what had happened. I must have then fainted again in bed.

The next day, I woke up. By then I realized what had happened. My family was still there again with me.

"Don't worry Miyuki. You have been under a lot of pressure with your two jobs. We think that you need a good, long rest. You need to come back with us to Morioka."

They did not of course know the full story. But I agreed to go with them. "I have had enough of Tokyo. I need to go back home. I need some peace and quiet."

Mimi

I was terribly shaken. My mother had left my father to live with her French boyfriend in Paris. My father had committed suicide. Life in Japan was just not the same since my return from France. And Eddie, the man who had breathed hope and dreams into my life had run away to live in a monastery. We didn't have the same intimacy as before.

"And now, following the 11 March Tohoku-Kanto Great Disaster, we have descended into a massive nuclear energy disaster. While the earthquake and tsunami are genuine tragedies, the nuclear disaster is without doubt the result of incompetence and corruption from our business and government leaders."

I had to do something. The only thing I could think of was going away again, but for a longer period of time. I had to sort out my mind and feelings.

Where could I go to? I could return to France and work for Jean, my mother's boyfriend. But I didn't want to be dependent on my mother and Jean. Also, I no longer had any confidence in my relationship with Eddie. While France is a beautiful country, with a wonderful culture, traditions and history, it is too similar to Japan in many ways. It does not offer its youth any future, opportunities or hope.

I need to go somewhere with hope and opportunity, with an open society and dynamic economy. There is only one choice, that is China. What's more China and Japan are two countries which are destined to live together.

Relations might be bad between our countries now. According to the latest opinion polls, some 80 per cent of Japanese do not trust the Chinese people. And Japan's politicians are not helping things. But this cannot go on forever. We must learn to live together.I decided to go to China to learn the Chinese language and discover this country's magnificent civilization.

I invited my two closest friends -- Eddie and Sandy -- over to my apartment, which since the departure of my mother and death of my father, had really become my apartment. I wanted to talk with them, get their opinions and advice. I also just wanted to see them again. Since Sandy has been married and living in Nigata, I had not really seen her.

Same goes for Eddie since he has been in the monastery. My relationship with Eddie seemed to be fading. Japanese often understand such things by telepathy, we call it "ishin denshin", heart-to-heart. I knew that Eddie had drifted away.

Eddie

When I arrived at the front gate of Mimi's apartment, someone else arrived at the same time. It was Sandy, the Chinese masseur. We were both shocked to see each other. We both remembered each other very clearly from the massage parlor.

Sandy's erotic massage was the mother of all climaxes. I could also sense that for Sandy, I was no ordinary massage customer.

We quickly deduced that we were both going to the same place. We touched other's hands as a sign of the intense feeling that we have for each other. We were both blushing and could feel the heat rise up through our necks. Spontaneously, we both waited, instinctively knowing that we must cool down before we enter Mimi's apartment.

When we entered, we sat down opposite one another. Mimi was full of self assurance and fully occupied with her own concerns. She explained to us both her state of mind, her need for a fresh start and her intention of going to China.

We agreed to have dinner at a Chinese restaurant. With Mimi having unburdened her heart, we all started talking freely. Sandy was flattered that Mimi should be going to China. I didn't comment on her plans. I felt strangely non-communicative. I think that Mimi could feel something strange in the air, an intimate vibration. Could she sense that Sandy and I know each other?

When we left the restaurant, Sandy and I headed off in the direction of the metro. We tried to hide our feelings until Mimi was out of sight. But at one point it was too much. Our hands grazed seemingly spontaneously, and then Sandy grabbed my hands tightly. Mimi was off in the distance by this time, too far away to see us. But perhaps through telepathy, she could feel our intimacy. Way in the distance, we could hear uncontrollable sobbing.

Walking towards the metro, Sandy and I passed near a love hotel. We looked at each other, and without saying a word we entered the front door. As soon as we entered the room, we undressed each other and kissed every millimeter of each other's body. Sandy pulled me on top of her and we entered a night of wild passion that would not end until day light.

The next morning that we departed our separate ways to the monastery and Nigata.

Sandy

One morning, when I get up I couldn't see Makoto on the floor in his usual position. There was not even any sign of him in the house.

I looked outside the kitchen window, and there he was in the garden, lying prostrate. He did not seem to be moving. As I walked over and looked at him, I could see that his skin was rather blue. I placed my hand on his forehead. It was freezing.

I was torn between happiness and sadness. I had actually become somewhat attached to this silly old man. But living with him was becoming intolerable. Also, life in the farm in Niagata was becoming boring especially now that I have completed my thesis.

Who should I contact? I didn't know. I could only think to call the Chinese agency who arranged our marriage. One of their drivers came straight out. He had seen this before. He would deliver Makoto to the hospital, and inform the police station. The Chinese agency seemed to have good relations with them all. It really made me wonder. I had actually read that the yakuza, Japan's famous mafia, was being gradually pushed out of some areas by the Chinese mafia who would make bigger payments to the police than the yakuza could afford.

What should I do now? I didn't know if I had fallen in too deep with the agency or not. I went to see the man who organized my marriage to Makoto. We had a long talk.

Eddie

It is Saturday morning. I am lying in bed in a Tokyo capsule hotel at the moment reading some manga magazines. Although I can't understand Japanese, I now buy Japanese language versions and try to imagine the story from the pictures. I love this because so many great Japanese manga have still not been translated into French.

The phone rings, and I answer it.

"Hi, it's Sandy here. Makoto's just died. What a relief to be rid of that old skunk. I will come down from Nigata this afternoon. Let's meet at Akihabara JR station."

"I have a great plan to share with you. My Chinese friends in Nigata would like to open an electronic goods shop in Akihabara to target the booming Chinese tourist market by selling counterfeit video games. They have a factory on the outskirts of Nigata which is hidden in an old rice farm."

"I will arrive at 5.40 this afternoon. I know a good Sichuan restaurant where I used to go. I am dying for a bowl of tan tan men."

Aiko

I am sitting here in the main restaurant at Zurich railway station drinking hot chocolate and eating chocolate torte cake. "No-one can beat those Swiss Germans for doing things just right", I thought to myself. "We Japanese might be perfectionists, but the Swiss Germans also have a lot of style and class".

I was so exhausted after a day of long and complex discussions with my bankers and lawyers. But everything is fixed now. Some Swiss German banks now offer special financial services to Japanese women who are in the process of divorcing their husbands. "It's amazing," I puzzled "how they master the art of financial secrecy and personal discretion".

My train for Paris would leave in twenty minutes time. So I telephoned Jean: "I will be arriving at the Gare de l'Est at 6.40 this afternoon. I am taking the train that goes through Basle. I can't wait to see you. Let's go somewhere nice for dinner tonight".

Mimi

I stumbled onto the Japan Airlines flight for Beijing. After some time, I eventually found my seat and my body just flopped into the place. I was totally exhausted after all the events and preparations for my departure. I was so happy to be leaving Tokyo behind.

Suddenly I do something so un-Japanese. I greet the young boy in the seat next to me and introduce myself. I didn't know what overcame me. A sudden sense of freedom and liberation perhaps.

He responded with perhaps the same sense of freedom and liberation:

"I am very pleased to meet you, my name is Hiddey."